As dawn came up over the Indian Ocean, the American girl standing at the rail of a steamer saw a volcano begin to erupt on a nearby island.

Or *was* it a volcano? For instead of an explosion of fire and lava, from the smoking crest of the mountain rose a shining cylinder, driven upward on a spear of flame. It was a space missile!

But who could be sending up a rocket from this deserted area? What was its purpose?

Suzie had no time to ponder this, for suddenly a second missile rose from the island. But this one was not aimed toward space—it was homing directly in on the steamer!

This is the 8th in Ace Books' series of exciting MAN FROM U.N.C.L.E. novels. For information on earlier books, see page 160.

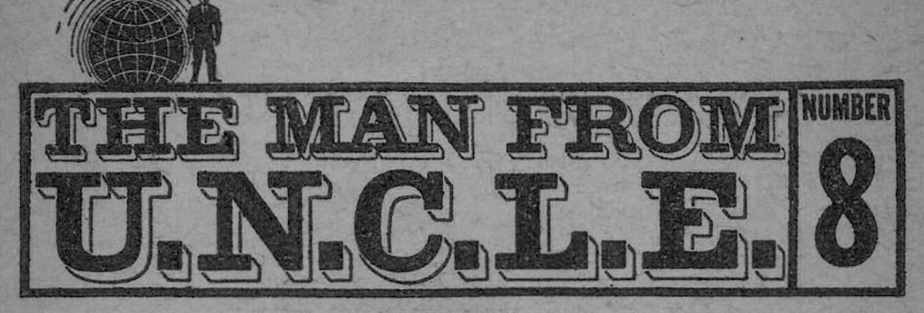

The Monster Wheel Affair

by David McDaniel.

Ace Books Inc.
1120 Avenue of the Americas
New York, N. Y. 10036

THE MONSTER WHEEL AFFAIR

DEDICATION:

To Ted Johnstone,
for ten years of unremitting labor
which put me where I am today.

Note: The Egypt in this narrative is entirely fictional, and has no relation to any real Egypt, living or dead.

Printed in U.S.A.

THE MONSTER WHEEL AFFAIR

DAWN WAS A GHOSTLY TINT of gold separating the sea from the sky. The stars were lost behind the brightening glow of the coming day, and the horizon was a flat circle with only a misty lump of distant island to break its perfection.

The tramp steamer *Paxton Merchant* extinguished her running lights as morning began to overtake her from astern. A new day of work was beginning for her crew, and a new day of pleasurable boredom for her half-dozen passengers.

Suzie Danz, 26, American, stood at the after rail on the bridge and checked over her camera. Three years' savings had gone into this trip, and she intended to capture everything possible on film. She had a plenitude of studies of shipboard life taken since their departure from Perth, but she had chosen this morning to rise early to view the Indian Ocean dawn, reputedly the most beautiful in the world. The weather had been inclement for the last few days, but this morning the sky was as clear as could be imagined.

She took a last light reading and set her camera towards the horizon above the fantail. Her long telephoto lens would magnify the first bright sliver of the sun, and her wide-angle lens stood ready to catch the splendid panorama of golden clouds and angel-eye blue which would herald the morning. She cocked the shutter.

Behind her, at the forward rail of the bridge, John MacKendricks squinted suddenly through the powerful binoculars which were at that moment focused on the nameless island some twenty-five miles ahead of them. Something was happening there. A cloud of smoke rose from the haze-shimmering mountain peak, and a flickering light illuminated it from below. A volcanic eruption?

He turned and called to the pretty photographer, whose attention was half a horizon away.

"Miss Danz! Come forward and look. There's a volcano going off up there!"

She only took a moment to react. After all, dawn happened every day, wherever you were. But volcanos were a special treat, and took priority. A glance at her light meter, and her telephoto-magnified viewfinder centered on the island as she braced the camera on the rail. She snapped the first shot, and then looked again.

"Look, Mac!" she said. "The smoke's getting thicker in the center. No . . ." She gasped, wound the film and fired again. "There's something coming out of the volcano!"

She got a third shot as something did indeed rise from the smoking crest of the distant mountain. To MacKendricks it seemed for a moment of disbelief like the neck of some impossible monster, rising straight up from a prehistoric hillside. Then the shape resolved into a shining cylinder. A fraction of a second later its base was clearly visible, and he squinted against the brilliance of the ravening waterfall of flame that drove it upward.

Suzie crouched, tilting and firing her camera at the thing as fast as she could wind and shoot. Then the sound began to reach them, faint over the watery distance. It was a familiar sound to a girl of the city, where jets crossed the sky dozens of times a day, but an alien one here, halfway around the world from her home. It was the roar of a continuous explosion—a rocket blast driving an intercontinental ballistic missile either on a test flight, on a sudden atomic attack, or on a space voyage. Whatever it was, it had no place here, far from the world's centers of international conflict and scientific research.

The rocket left a writhing white track behind it as it drove up through the stratosphere, and became no more than a glittering speck in the camera's viewfinder, catching the sun. Suzie wound one more time, and felt the advance lever stick as it pulled at the end of the film. She looked up at last and was slightly surprised to find she could hardly see the vapor trail a few miles above them. She started to rewind the film as she looked around for MacKendricks.

Mac was no longer there. He was inside the wheelhouse in excited converse with the steersman, Kurt Schneider.

"Did you pick that up on the navigational radar?"

Kurt nodded. "*Ja.* It was a missile. Did you see it?"

"Sure did, and I think Miss Danz got some pictures of it. What island is that, anyway? Got it on the chart?"

Kurt turned and bent over a large map. "I make our position here," he said slowly. "This would be the island." His closed dividers touched their slightly bent points to a speck on the chart. "There is no warning notice here—but this is an old chart. Perhaps I should suggest the Captain write it in himself."

MacKendricks grunted agreement, while privately reserving his opinion as to the public knowledge on any chart concerning this little island. The *Paxton Merchant* was a good many miles north of the regular shipping lane, as their course from Perth was not directly to Capetown, but to Tamatave. This island might not be seen by a ship from one year to the next.

He looked again at the little green screen of the radar, where the shape of the island glowed near the top. Then he looked more closely and pointed. "What's that?"

"That" was a speck of green that had detached itself from the larger mass and was moving directly down the face of the tube towards the central dot that represented the ship. Kurt watched it for a few seconds while the pale green radius swept once around the face of the tube. Then the speck was visibly closer.

"*Donnerwetter!*" he said as he jumped for a panel high on the wall. His fingers flipped aside the red metal cover and his palm slapped against the red button. Instantly a clangorous alarm went off all over the ship. Kurt grabbed the log book from its case and ran for the door of the wheelhouse.

"In the absence of Captain I take command," he barked to three sailors who appeared, unshaven and half dressed. "Lower boats—right now!"

MacKendricks grabbed his arm. "What *was* that?"

"Either a jet plane or a rocket launched from the island. In two minutes we could be blown out of the water!"

The emergency alarm hammered its hysterical monotone as the nearest boat was swung out over the water. MacKendricks grabbed Suzie, who grabbed her camera case, and threw her into the boat as it was being lowered. One by one sleep-dazed heads began appearing as crewmen stumbled on deck. The Captain himself stepped out, struggling into a bathrobe.

"Schneider," he bawled, "what the hell is all this?"

"We are under attack, sir, and may be hit in a minute or two. There is not time to explain."

"Take command here—I'll rouse the passengers." The Captain turned and dived down a hatch.

The first boat, with Suzie in it, hit the water. Mac and three other sailors were in it with her—how they'd got there, she couldn't tell. Someone started the motor, and they began to pull away from the ship.

Suddenly the Captain reappeared on deck, as a second boat rocked out on its davits, and he ordered Schneider in along with several people Suzie recognized as her fellow passengers.

Then Mac pointed and shouted. Suzie looked up.

Something fat and stubby-winged appeared in the distance, growing larger. "Everybody lie down flat and hold onto something," Mac commanded. "And pray as hard as you ever did in your life."

Suzie had to look over the side of the boat, and as she did so she was the only one to see clearly what happened.

The rocket struck high, well above the waterline, but directly in the center of the ship, aft of the bridge. For an instant there was only a ragged hole. Then from the depths of the ship came a puff of flame, and a wave of concussion pounded her face. It was followed by a muffled roar, and a billow of fire swept up from a great tear across the center of the ship. A moment later it had broken in half and was already starting to sink. Of the men who had stood on her decks a few seconds before Suzie could see nothing. Part of a shattered lifeboat hung from one burning rope, and as she watched, her eyes fixed on the horrible scene by shock, the rope parted and dropped the wrecked prow of the boat into the water.

A series of explosions came now from both halves of the hulk as the waves rose swiftly around them. The motor of the little lifeboat chattered desperately as it drove away from the sucking swirl of water that tried to pull them down with the ship.

At last the great bubbles stopped and the roiling surface calmed. And only wreckage remained, gummed and surrounded in a wide and spreading black oil slick—the life blood of the ship, gushing forth as she sank into the endless night below.

TABLE OF CONTENTS

Section I: "The Sailor Told Me Before He Died . . ."

Chapter 1

"A Dollar A Round."

THE CABLEGRAM FROM Capetown was addressed simply UNCLEHQNYC. It arrived in the east-side Manhattan offices of the United Network Command for Law and Enforcement on a Tuesday morning, and was brought directly to the desk of Alexander Waverly. The message was terse and cryptic:

IMPORTANT BUSINESS DEAL. SEND NEPHEW IMMEDIATELY. PHOTOGRAPHS FOLLOW. MACKENDRICKS.

Waverly read it again. The return address was the Voortrek Hotel, Capetown, South Africa. The meaning of the cable was clear enough, but . . . He touched a panel at his elbow.

"Do we have a file on anyone named MacKendricks who might be sending us a report from South Africa?"

The voice answered immediately. "Yes, sir. A Mr. MacKendricks has supplied us with information from several quarters of the world almost a dozen times in the last fifteen years. I'll bring his file in."

"Very good. And page Mr. Solo and Mr. Kuryakin."

"Yes, sir."

The little pistol looked like a toy made of stamped tin, and felt like one in his hand as Napoleon Solo leveled it at the brightly-lighted target fifty feet away. *Trigger's a little stiff,* he thought as he squeezed it gently. There was the slight jar of the hammer striking, a burst of fire from the vents along the barrel, and a puff of heat over his hand, arm and face. With a sound like a starched handkerchief being ripped, amplified many times, a faint trail of smoke zipped out of the gun and ended halfway to the far wall. The noise echoed around the concrete walls of the basement range for a few seconds before vanishing into the acoustic tile.

The rangemaster squinted through the little spotting scope. "Not bad," he said. "Five ring at seven o'clock."

Napoleon squinted. A terrible shot, considering his usual accuracy. He consciously relaxed his hand, which had tensed to receive the recoil which had never come, and centered his sights on the black circle.

Another sharp spitting shot, and another puff of heat. And the laconic voice saying, "Seven ring at six o'clock."

He was shooting low; time to apply Tennesee windage. He drew a careful bead a couple of inches above the distant bullseye and fired a third time. This time there was a pause as the rangemaster searched the target. "Just outside the five ring at one-thirty."

Napoleon set the safety, lowered his right hand and flexed his fingers after laying the weapon on the bench. A soft voice spoke behind him.

"I see you've found the new toy. What do you think?"

He turned to see Illya, hands in the pockets of an acid-stained lab smock, regarding him and the Gyrojet pistol.

He started to speak, but Illya continued: "Tell me on the way upstairs. We have been summoned to Mr. Waverly's office. Save the rest of the magazine," he added as Napoleon started to reach for the rocket pistol. "At a dollar a round, someone else can use the practice."

In the elevator, as Napoleon ran a quick comb through his hair and straightened his tie, Illya said, "I tried the Gyrojet as soon as it came in. A good idea, but the pistol is quite inaccurate."

"Accurate enough," said Napoleon, as he checked his appearance in a polished metal panel. "Even at fifty feet all three of those slugs would have connected. And at close range accuracy wouldn't matter."

"But at close range it has no striking power," said the Russian. "It takes twenty-five feet for the rocket projectile to achieve maximum velocity. I prefer the more traditional 9 mm parabellums we use."

"There's no recoil at all," said Napoleon. "If the barrel were longer, or the burning time shorter, it'd be more accurate."

"The whole reason for a gun," said Illya flatly, as the door slid open and they stepped out, "is to put a little piece of metal exactly where you want it when you want it there. Anything that fails in this purpose fails as a gun."

"But suppose you want to put it there without attracting undue attention," said his partner. "The rocket pistol is a lot quieter than an ordinary gun. And suppose you wanted to shoot something underwater—the Gyrojet works as well there as in the air."

"Yes, and every bit as accurately, too," said Illya. "If I ever go shooting for whales, I may take one."

"I tell you what," said Napoleon. "Next assignment we go on, I'll carry the Gyrojet and you carry your U.N.C.L.E. Special. And we'll see which one comes in handier."

They stopped at Mr. Waverly's door, as he added, "And come to think of it, it's not a bad murder gun—no ballistic marks on the bullet."

"I don't think they'd stop to look for them," said Illya, with his slight smile, "if you are the only man in the country who owns one."

Napoleon looked at him consideringly for a moment, and finally said, "Are you going to take off that lab coat, or do you want to impress him with your tireless industry?"

Illya glanced down, startled, and the corner of his mouth twitched in mild embarrassment. He quickly slipped out of the coat and handed it to the secretary, who accepted it without a flicker of reaction.

He stepped through the door after his partner and felt rather than heard it slide closed behind him.

Waverly looked up from a file folder as they took their seats at the round table which dominated the office. "A cablegram arrived from South Africa this morning," he said, as Solo picked up the yellow flimsy and held it so his partner could read.

A moment later Illya looked up. "Who's MacKendricks?"

"John Calvin MacKendricks," said Waverly, "is third officer on the *Paxton Merchant*, a tramp freighter which sailed from Perth about a month ago. He has no official position with U.N.C.L.E., but has been the source of useful information to us a few times in the past. A trustworthy man, with neither home nor family outside of his ship. Now he is an orphan and a widower—the *Paxton Merchant* was reported sunk a week ago by a ship which picked up a single lifeboat. MacKendricks, four other crewmen, and an American girl who had been a passenger were the only survivors. They said there must have been a boiler explosion.

"It now appears something of extreme importance is involved. If I did not trust MacKendricks' evaluation, I would simply turn the data over to the African office—either the local branch in Capetown or the Continental Office in Addis Ababa. But they lack the facilities for a problem of international scope, and are fully occupied keeping the African situation from getting any worse. Because of this probable importance, Mr. Solo, you will fly to Capetown via London tomorrow morning. You, Mr. Kuryakin, will follow him in a few days with the information contained in the photographs which are supposed to be on their way here. Any questions?"

"Several," said Napoleon. "What am I supposed to do in Capetown?"

"Evaluate the situation. Meet Mr. MacKendricks and

find out what he is being so secretive about. If the problem warrants our action, proceed at will. If not, turn it over to U.N.C.L.E. Capetown. We have problems enough in our own bailiwick to occupy our attention."

"Ah, one more thing—I would like permission to add an extra weapon to my kit."

"What?"

"The Gyrojet. Any weapon that radical should be extensively field tested by trained personnel before thought is given to its adoption into the armory."

"And you want to play with it for a while. Very well. But remember it is still untested. Don't trust your life to it in a tight spot." He turned to Illya. "By the way, that reminds me. How did your experimentation with the smaller version of the rocket work out?"

Napoleon glanced at his partner with a slightly raised eyebrow, as the Russian said, "Inconclusive. The Fin-jets seem to have a great deal of potential; easily concealable, fairly accurate, and quite deadly. In fact, I have one concealed here." He pulled the older model communicator out of his coat pocket, and opened the side of it which doubled as a cigarette case. He selected the end cigarette, and held it out. It was a filter-tip, indistinguishable from the others.

"The fuse extends to the front," he said, pointing, "where it is concealed behind a quarter inch of tobacco." He placed the cigarette between his lips and pantomimed striking a match. Talking around the filter, he continued, "The fuse ignites when the cigarette has burned to this point. Five seconds later it has burned the length of the Fin-jet, inside the tobacco, and the little missile fires. The filter tip protects the user from the back-blast, and sighting is not difficult."

Napoleon murmured, "Caution: cigarette smoking may be hazardous to the next guy's health."

Waverly smiled. "This interest in technical advances in our weaponry is heartening, but don't be tempted into finding excuses to try them out. On an ideal mission, not even a temper is ruffled. The ends of secrecy are best served by stealth."

"Now about Capetown . . ." said Napoleon.

"Everything is here," said Waverly, placing a small manila folder on the table and giving it a turn towards his agent. "Address of the hotel where MacKendricks is staying, picture of him—it's ten years old, but I don't imagine he'll have changed much—passport, proper visa, and ticket."

Napoleon looked at the items, checking them over, and tucked them into various pockets.

"One last thing," added his superior. "I would appreciate a call at your earliest convenience regarding your decision on the matter. We could save Mr. Kuryakin a trip to Capetown."

Chapter 2

"An Awfully Big Haystack."

UNDER THE CIRCUMSTANCES, Napoleon did not check in with U.N.C.L.E. Capetown as soon as he arrived. He caught a cab directly from the airport to the center of town and the Voortrek Hotel. The desk clerk gave him a room number and a house phone, and a minute later a cautious voice said, "Yes?"

"Uncle Mac? This is your nephew, Napoleon Solo, from New York. I was told you might be able to use my help in a business deal, so I flew right in."

"Good. We've been expecting you. Come on up and . . ." MacKendricks paused suddenly as if listening for something, then added, ". . . and hurry!"

Mac dropped the phone in its cradle, picked up a lumpy old revolver and stepped to the door into the next room. He listened there closely, then turned to the window. He teased aside the edge of one drawn drape and looked out. No one there. Now, had he heard a footstep, or hadn't he? He checked the door into the corridor, feeling like a foolish old man looking for burglars.

Out in the corridor were four burglars. All stamped from the same mold: large, husky, and mean-looking. One of them tapped lightly on the next door—Suzie's. They didn't look as if they were selling encyclopedias, Mac decided, but if they were, you'd better buy.

He closed the door very softly and slipped on the chain, then hurried to the adjoining door. He opened it, saying, "Suzie girl, don't open . . ." But her hand was already on the knob and turning, as she looked back over her shoulder with mild surprise. And then it was too late.

A broad shoulder slammed against the door, tearing it from Suzie's grip and throwing it wide open. The first pair had bulky automatics in their fists and were already looking around for something to use them on.

As the door burst open, Mac yelled, "Get down, Suzie!" And then the room was filled with the thunder of his revolver and the sharp sweet smell of gunpowder. Suzie felt something pluck at her hair as she dived for the slight amount of cover afforded by the sofa, and the slamming bark of an automatic made her ears ring.

Napoleon Solo heard the gunfire as he stepped out of the elevator. His own U.N.C.L.E. Special was in his hand as he sprinted the length of the hall, and it took him only a moment to decide on which side his loyalties lay. One dark-suited man sat against a wall, an automatic near his limp hand and a spreading stain across his chest. Napoleon fired twice, and had the satisfaction of seeing another pistol fall to the floor as its erstwhile owner ceased to care about anything.

The two remaining men leaped behind things as Napoleon ducked back behind the doorframe. He should have used the two shots he'd had time for to wing two instead of killing one, he thought belatedly. But his momentary survey of the scene of action had also shown him an old man lying in an open doorway, and he had been a little upset. He also wondered what had become of the girl.

He found out a moment later, as a rough and heavily accented voice called, "Hey, Mister! We got the girl, and she's coming out with us. You hear?"

Napoleon hoped the girl was small—it's hard to hide behind someone much smaller than you, and he could get in the one shot that would count if he had half a chance and just a piece of target.

"Keep your gun down, and stand away from the door, hear me?"

Solo gave back a reluctant monosyllabic acknowledgment, and let his pistol hang at the end of his arm as he stepped back a couple of paces.

A moment later an angry little figure, unmistakably feminine, was rudely propelled into the corridor at the end of an anonymous arm which gripped her wrist firmly. She looked both ways, and saw Napoleon. Before either of them could say hello, she was joined by her chaperone, dark-visaged, moustached, and armed. He pulled her tightly to him as a shield, and directed the snout of a still-smoking automatic over her right shoulder. Napoleon suppressed a slight smile as he saw she only came up to the man's chin, and his wrist muscles tensed slightly as he estimated the placement of the single shot he would have time for.

The next moment a second man, almost a twin of the first but thinner, stepped out of the door. He too held an automatic, its muzzle directed steadily towards Napoleon's center of gravity. Solo cursed his hesitation—he should have dropped the first one before the second came out. But then the girl might have been shot from cover. Valuable to U.N.C.L.E. she might be, but at the moment she was a definite liability to one particular agent. Helpless females were fun in their place, but encountering one on the job was certainly not. . . .

Suddenly the helpless female under consideration became a brief blur of action. She brought her heel down violently on her captor's instep and jabbed her free elbow halfway to the wrist in his stomach. As his face contorted and he doubled over, his automatic exploded beside her ear and the slug tore a gouge in the wall inches from Napoleon's gun hand—or where his hand would have been if his reactions had been a little slower.

He snapped into action the moment he saw the girl begin to move, and had evaluated the situation in the fraction of a second it took him to bring his pistol level and squeeze the trigger. The big one was doubling over, his mouth open like a beached fish. The second one had turned his head and started to swing his gun towards his companion. It was perfectly simple, and Solo took advantage of it.

The second assassin probably never knew what hit him. Under the circumstances Napoleon knew better than to try circus stunts like shooting him in the hand. He drilled him once through the chest, and without a twinge watched his body leap back under the impact and flop against the wall before sliding to the floor. Before he hit, the U.N.C.L.E. Special was centered on the last of the invaders, who was doubled over against the other wall, his face an interesting shade of purple behind the moustache.

The girl was getting slowly up from the floor, shaking her head weakly and rubbing at her right ear. Napoleon knelt beside her and slipped a supporting hand under her arm.

"You all right?" he asked.

"I think so," she said hesitantly, "except it'll be a while before I'll be able to hear clearly again. Golly, that thing makes a racket!"

"Before we get any more involved in mayhem, allow me to introduce myself. I'm Napoleon Solo, from New

York. Do you happen to know . . . Excuse me a moment."

The lone survivor of the attack group was moving feebly across the floor towards an automatic. Napoleon slipped the magazine out of his own pistol, fumbled in an inner pocket, and popped something into the open chamber. He pointed the weapon at the man as the girl screwed her face up and turned her head away.

There was a *chuff*, and the man stopped moving. A moment later the girl looked around hesitantly.

"Oh, he's not dead," said Solo. "But he'll sleep peacefully until we decide what to do with him. It may be a problem—his type does not usually respond well to rehabilitation and retraining. But as I was saying," he continued as he replaced the magazine in his U.N.C.L.E. Special and worked the slide to bring a cartridge into the chamber, "do you know a gentleman named MacKendricks? I came here to meet him."

Her face changed suddenly. "Oh dear heavens! Mac!" she gasped, and jumped for the door of the room.

Napoleon looked up and down the hall, and shook his head slowly. He would never cease to be amazed at the things one could get away with in public places without attracting attention. Well, it was all right with *him* if people didn't want to get involved. He wedged his automatic back into its cozy holster and set to work clearing the corridor of corpses.

The sleeping one he dragged by the legs into the room, and looked around for the girl. Then he dropped him and stepped quickly to where she knelt by a gray-haired man who lay on the floor, a great dark stain oozing slowly through the rug around him.

Napoleon knelt beside her as the old man opened his eyes. "Mr. MacKendricks—my name is Solo. From U.N.C.L.E. Headquarters."

The eyes turned to focus on him. "Have y' seen th' pictures?"

"No—I started as soon as your cable arrived. The film hadn't come in yet."

"Somebody's got a rocket base in the Indian Ocean—a big one. I thought you'd better know. Somebody else thought you'd better not, I guess." He chuckled a little, and coughed. Flecks of red appeared around his lips.

"Oh, Mac, don't talk!" said the girl desperately. "We've got to get you to a doctor!"

"Hush now, Suzie girl. I haven't got more than a bit of time, and I've got to think. I knew the location of the island—I can't think. You, Mr.—"

"Solo."

"Of course. You, find Kurt. He was navigator. He was with us. He and I—we knew the coördinates. We were a long way short of Madagascar—twenty-something-something south. . . . Can't think."

Suzie stifled a sob, and Mac lifted a hand to touch her shoulder. "Now stop that, girl. It doesn't hurt at all, now. And I've done just about everything else in this world. But I've got to tell you—stay with Mr. Solo. He's one of the best men in the world, and he's got a gold card to prove it. Ask him what U.N.C.L.E. means. You'll be safer with him than anywhere else. As for you, Mr. Solo—find Kurt Schneider. He was going to hide someplace, but you can find him before those others. And just one last thing—a favor I'd ask of you."

Napoleon nodded.

"Have me buried at sea. I've spent my whole life cheatin' the ocean, and it wouldn't be fair to let the land take me away from her forever."

"I promise."

"And take care of Suzie—she's as dear to me as a daughter. She can tell you everything but the location of that damned island." His face drew up into a vague frown. "One of us knew besides me—who was it?"

"Kurt," said Suzie gently. "Kurt Schneider."

"That's right. Kurt. A brave man, staying on the ship like that until the Captain took over. I remember that. The ship blew up just after his boat got off. We thought he was killed. A brave man he was. Find him, Suzie, and find that island." His eyes closed, and his breath rasped in his throat as his hand gripped weakly at her shoulder. Her lips paled, but she held her emotion in.

Napoleon saw her eyes shine with tears a moment, just before the hand slipped from her shoulder and fell across the old man's chest. Her whole body was quivering as Napoleon slipped a comforting arm around her.

Then she turned suddenly to him, tears streaming down her cheeks, and released her anguish. Her hands on his shoulders, her face pressed against his chest, she sobbed convulsively for some time.

Solo guessed that some of her reaction was to the violence she had been a part of only a few minutes before, and decided it would be a good thing for her to clear it out of her system. But on the other hand, there were a few more things to be done.

He helped her to her feet, and got her over to the couch. She slumped there, tear-drops staining the dark cloth until it seemed the same color as the rug around the body of the old man, who still lay where he had fallen in her defense.

Meanwhile, Napoleon was busy dragging the rest of the bodies into the room. *Neatness is a virtue,* he thought to himself as he arranged them along the wall in order of size. *Besides, if we left them out in the hall, some bellboy would stumble over them eventually, and he might not understand at all.* He stopped to consider this thought. *I wonder,* he said to himself, *if I might not be getting a little callous towards death.*

His next action was to check in with home base. Channel D put him in direct communication with Waverly, by way of an automatic local relay station and the nearest communications satellite, where it was beamed to New York, multiplexed on an apparently innocent carrier. It was a matter of seconds before the familiar gruff voice inquired impatiently as to what the problem seemed to be.

Solo gave him a complete report on the attempted—and half successful—assassination. By the time he had finished, the whole situation was clearer in his own mind for having been verbalized. His receiver was silent for several seconds.

"Your promise to MacKendricks makes it awkward," came the voice at last. "It would be simpler to take the girl and leave all the bodies behind. Can you get his body out undetected?"

"It'd be easier if I had some help, sir. And it appears now there's nothing in this that directly affects the local office, so I'd like your permission to call them in. I'll need some fairly complex investigating facilities too, to trace Schneider. And then there's the Sleeping Beauty, too. I doubt if the local law would know what to do with him."

"Permission granted," said the voice over seven thousand miles of ocean. "Those photographs haven't been seen here yet—find out if this girl knows anything about them."

Suzie was staring at the little silver tube, tear-streaks drying unnoticed on her cheeks. Now she sat up and held out a hand. "Here," she said unsteadily. "Let me talk to him."

She fumbled with it for a moment, locating the microphone. "Hello?" she said tentatively.

"Who is this?"

"My same is Suzanne Danz, of Chicago. I was on the *Paxton Merchant* when she was attacked and sunk by an unknown power. Mister MacKendricks saved my life then, and he saved it again today."

"I helped," said Napoleon under his breath, but she didn't hear.

"What are these photographs?" Waverly asked.

"I took almost a whole roll of pictures with a telephoto lens just before the ship was blown up. They were of a big rocket being launched from an island. Mac and Kurt were the only ones who knew the position we were at when we saw the rocket. Kurt stayed on the ship until the Captain ordered him off just before the bomb hit. We thought he'd been killed too but Mac saw him floating in the oil slick and pulled him in and we were just able to get him breathing again—we thought he'd been killed by the concussion but Mac saved his life too and now he's dead and they shot him . . ."

Her voice was rising in pitch and she was breathing harder. Napoleon reached forward and gripped her arm hard. She stopped short and squeezed her eyes tight shut.

"Look," he said intently. "You've had a rough time, and it may be a while before it's all over. But you're as safe as you can be now. Mac is dead, but he died the best way a man can. And the best thing you can do now is stay calm and help us all you can. Okay?"

She nodded mutely, but didn't open her eyes. Napoleon gently removed the transmitter from her clenched fist.

"Mr. Waverly? Sorry for the interruption. A touch of reaction. Send Illya down as soon as those pictures come in. I'll get in contact with U.N.C.L.E. Capetown and give them a song-and-dance about why I'm here without their knowledge. Anything else?"

"Nothing, as long as you continue to justify my faith in you. You can take care of yourself. Do so."

"Thank you, sir." Why was it Waverly always made an explicit statement of his confidence when conditions were worst? Oh well, it usually worked, and that was justification enough.

He thumbed the call button again, and requested Channel L.

Forty-five very busy minutes later he and Suzie were sitting in a neatly furnished office. The single survivor of the unsuccessful attack was being received downstairs by U.N.C.L.E.'s medical technicians, and prepared for a thorough interrogation which he would not even remember the next day. Also downstairs was the body which had once belonged to John Calvin MacKendricks, awaiting disposal in accord with his last wishes.

Upstairs Suzie Danz leaned back in a metal chair and addressed a microphone. "Well, we found Kurt Schneider floating in the oil, and after we pulled him in we looked around for a while, but there wasn't anybody else. And I guess that was about all."

"All right," said Napoleon. "What happened after that?"

"Nothing much. Well, the boat was stocked for eight, but we didn't have a radio. So we put up a sail and went south until Mac and Kurt thought we were in the main shipping lane, and then drifted around for seven days until we were spotted and found. Kurt took command, with Mac as his first mate, and set up food and water rationing. We had enough for another four days when the *Ballyshannon* took us aboard."

She smiled suddenly. "I lost everything except for my camera and my lenses and film. And I've got about six rolls of life in a lifeboat. I used a wide-angle, mostly, and I photographed just about everything. Maybe I can sell it to *Life* or *National Geographic*. I sent the film off after we got here, except for the roll I shot of the missile taking off. Mac took that. He said it was very important that it got directly to the right people, and he'd be sure it did." She looked at Napoleon. "I guess you're the right people."

Napoleon nodded. "We're going to need your help to find the other men who were in that lifeboat with you. Are you willing to work with us for a while?"

"I'm willing to go anywhere and do anything, for as long as it takes to get whoever is behind this. They murdered that ship and everybody on her, and they murdered Mac and tried to get me too. I'll say I'm willing to work with you!"

"Good." He leaned forward, stopped the tape recorder, and picked up the handset of a telephone with a flashing light in place of its dial. As he did so the light stopped flashing.

"Solo. . . . Good. Who's missing?" He scowled. "Figures. What about the other three?" He covered the mouthpiece momentarily and addressed Suzie. "Three of your shipmates have been traced already. Schneider is the only one we don't have a line on yet." He turned back to the telephone. "Good. Go ahead."

He repeated aloud, for her benefit: "Archie Gunderson signed on the *Miyako Maru,* bound for Hong Kong. We can meet him there. Alexei Kropotkin shipped out two days later for Rio de Janeiro on the *Duke of York.* Waleed al-Fadly . . ." His face fell slightly, but he continued: ". . . is beyond our reach. He was found knifed in an alley by the waterfront just last night. We'll have to move quickly to get to Gunderson and Kropotkin before the other side does." He addressed the telephone again. "Keep trying to trace Schneider. He's apparently the only one who can give us that location now.

"By the way, what about our guest downstairs? Have you found out his home port?" He listened, and nodded slowly. "Local boy, hired through channels for a routine kill. Not a chance of back-tracking him, either, I suppose. Okay—call me if anything comes up." He replaced the handset.

"My partner will be here in a few days," he said. "Then we will go off to Rio and Hong Kong, and see if Kurt may have told his erstwhile shipmates anything that could lead to his being found." He shook his head. "It's going to be quite a search if he didn't. The world is an awfully big haystack to lose one needle in."

Chapter 3

"What Did You Expect—Big Ben?"

THE JET THUNDERED down out of the deep blue South African sky. Below, Napoleon Solo and Suzie Danz stood in air-conditioned coolness listening to the muted sounds of airplanes outside the double glass windows and the metallic voice of a loudspeaker announcing the arrival of the flight from London. Illya was on that flight, and tucked in his bags were enlargements in full glorious color of a mysterious ICBM that had been launched a few weeks before.

Wheels smoked as braked tires vaporized against rubber-scarred concrete, and thrust-reversers drove the engines to an anguished scream. The BOAC jet rolled into the taxiway, slowing gently now, and crept at last into its berth. With a final sigh, the engines whined down to a stop.

Napoleon and Suzie met Illya at the gate as he checked through customs. The sight of the diplomatic passport he wielded won instant coöperation from the guards, and a small trolly with a rather remarkable assortment of bags wheeled past them unchallenged.

Solo looked from the cart and the sweating redcap who propelled it to his partner. "What did you do," he asked under his breath, "bring all of Section Three with you?"

"Just a few necessities," said Illya casually, directing his native bearer towards the line of taxis with a wave of his hand. "In this uncertain world, you never know what you might need."

It took two taxis to get them back to the hotel. Determined not to involve local U.N.C.L.E. operations any more than necessary, and certain that the center of the enemy's interest had left Capetown with the departure of Kurt Schneider, they had assumed the roles of normal tourists. *Almost* normal—Suzie was under armed guard at all times, courtesy of the Solo Personal Protection Bureau.

The three of them huddled over Illya's briefcase, which he had hand-carried rather than leave with the rest of the luggage. Unsnapping the trick fasteners, he gently raised the lid and withdrew a large manila envelope.

"Here are your prints," he said, handing it to Suzie. "Sorry I couldn't bring back the original slides, but they're in a safe place. Perhaps sometime we can get them back to you."

She carefully undid the metal clasp and slipped out a thin stack of glossy color prints, eight by ten. In the center of each frame was a long thin white object which grew shorter, print by print, as well as less distinct. She examined them, one at a time. Then her face lightened. "Oh, of course. Foreshortening as it went higher. And that's why it gets grainier. Bigger enlargements."

Illya nodded. "These are blown up as much as possible without an inordinate loss of detail." He turned to Napoleon. "Section Three was most interested in the design of this missile. They say it's roughly two hundred feet long, diameter in proportion. If the frames were shot about a second apart, it was accelerating at some 300 feet per second per second, or a bit less than ten gees. But what really aroused comment were the differences here"—he pointed to the main stage of the rocket, clearly visible in the third picture—"and here." He pointed to the second stage, and slid his finger up to the nose.

Napoleon looked at them closely, and knitted a thoughtful pair of eyebrows. "That's odd," he said finally, and Illya nodded.

"That's what they said, too."

Suzie put down the pile of prints she held, and looked over their shoulders. "What's odd?" she asked. "It looks like a common, ordinary ICBM to me."

"How many ICBM's have you known personally?"

"Well, not that many. But I've watched them on TV, and I've seen pictures of them. What makes this one so unusual, outside of being where it shouldn't be?"

"Can you tell the difference between, say, an Atlas-Agena and a Saturn Five?"

"Not unless I can see their license plates."

"Okay. These upper two stages are very much like the Agena—not exactly, but very much. Close enough that it's probably a patent infringement, if it matters. But this bottom stage is, as near as anyone can tell without poking around in the plumbing, the main stage from a Russian T 3-A, which is, frankly, more powerful than anything but our Saturn-V."

Illya nodded agreement. "Somebody has taken the best of both cultures and combined them. This may have been only a test, or it may have put something into orbit. Whichever it was, this combination is most practical, and potentially dangerous as a weapon."

The doorbell rang across the moment of silence that followed this statement. On the other side of the door, a winded team of bellhops was discovered standing beside a pile of luggage. Illya beckoned them in, watched while they bore their burdens into the room and set them about on the floor, on chairs and on the bed, and finally rewarded each of them with a crisp note of unseen but generous denomination.

Napoleon looked around at the stuff as the door closed again. "Well," he asked, "do we start to unpack, or do we divvy up the gear into portable lots before we take off for the far corners of the earth? Or do we just leave it here to startle the maid?"

"Golly," said Suzie, counting. "Ten, eleven, twelve bags. What all is in them, anyway?"

Illya's eyebrows raised slightly, and his gaze traveled smoothly around the room, checking the count. "I can tell you what is in eleven of them," he said. "Because that is how many I left New York with."

"Somebody else's bag must have gotten mixed in with yours by accident."

He shook his head. "In this business there are no accidents." He walked slowly among the luggage, looking at each item closely. He stopped by a small blue canvas bag, and put his ear up to it. A slight smile teased the corner of his mouth. "Marvellous." he said. "It's ticking."

Suzie gasped slightly, and cowered back against the nearest wall. "What are you going to do?"

"Disarm it, of course."

"Don't worry," said Napoleon reassuringly. "He's quite competent at this sort of thing. He's only had one bomb go off while he was working on it."

It took a moment for her to consider this, and then she looked hard at him. "And what happened? I suppose you'll tell me he was blown to bits?"

"Oh no—nothing happened. The bomb turned out to be a dud."

"It's quite true," said the soft voice from across the room. "But I can assure you I had a very bad fraction of a second there watching the detonator spark."

Suzie waited what seemed like a decent interval and then asked, "What are you going to do with this one—dunk it in water?"

"That went out several years ago. All the better time bombs these days are made with sodium metal in the detonator. Water will set them off before it renders the explosive harmless."

"In fact," said Napoleon, "it is quite possible to make a bomb so constructed that whatever you do to it in attempting to disarm it will set it off. Fortunately we haven't run into one yet."

Illya was feeling the bag very gently, and examining the zipper with a small magnifying lens. He shook his head slowly. "Quite true," he said. "For instance, I am fairly sure an attempt to open this zipper would result in detonation of the device."

Suzie looked at all the other bags and suitcases.

"Haven't you got something here that will take care of it?"

Napoleon shrugged. "We might be able to X-ray it to find out where everything is inside it—but we couldn't be sure that it might not be wired with a small fluorescent screen so the X-rays would trigger it."

"Oh," she said in a small voice, and looked doubtfully across the room at Illya. "Well, what *are* you going to do?"

"Probe," said the Russian succinctly, producing a long thin knife from somewhere.

He drew the tip of the knife over a short distance on the side of the bag, and continued to stroke the area like a surgeon making a life-and-death incision. Gradually the scratch deepened. In a few seconds a half-inch gash appeared in the canvas, and he stopped. "Excellent," he said softly, and folded the knife.

He turned, looking over the other bags scattered around the room, spotted one and nodded. From it he withdrew a flat metal box some twelve inches long. He crouched beside the ticking bag and opened the box.

The first thing he withdrew was a thin tube perhaps ten inches long, with a small cup at one end and an elastic band which Illya slipped over his head, adjusting the cup to one eye. He touched something beside the eyepiece, and the other end of the tube glowed softly. He slipped that end in through the incision.

"All right," Suzie whispered to Napoleon. "What's he doing now?"

"That's a proctoscope—a fiber-optic illuminator. Basically it's a light-pipe with a wide-angle lens and a tiny light on one end, and his eye at the other end. He can look all over the inside now."

Illya's visible eye, which had been closed, opened now and rolled over in the direction of the kit. His free hand slipped out something else long and thin.

"The rest of the kit," Napoleon continued, "is a surgical kit, essentially. Each gadget in there has something different on the end. A gripper, a knife blade, a shear . . . Surgeons use them for what they call 'keyhole' operations. They can work inside you through little holes; less tissue damage, less of a scar."

Suzie nodded. "When I had my appendix out a few years ago the scar was only about an inch long."

"What do you see in there?" Napoleon asked his partner.

"Wires—a couple of batteries—a large block of something—a timing mechanism . . ."

"Then it really *is* a bomb!" Suzie said.

"What did you expect—Big Ben?"

She paused, considering that, and decided to let it pass. "What are you doing now?"

"Clipping wires."

"Oh."

Illya worked in silence for a minute, then said, "This is a fairly sloppy job of bomb-making. The zipper was wired, as I thought, but it wouldn't have gone off if I'd opened it—one of the connections had broken loose. An amateurish job of soldering, too." He paused, manipulating his instruments through the tiny hole. "I think I want a closer look at those batteries. And that detonator mechanism . . ." He pulled out one tool, picked up another, and continued working. After a few seconds, he let out a long breath, and said, "That's it."

Napoleon took a step forward as Illya stood up slowly and slipped the eyepiece of the proctoscope off his head. "Let's see."

The Russian agent was replacing his tools in their case, fitting each slender, delicate instrument back in the proper clips, and finally closing the lid and fastening the catches. Only then did he slide the zipper tab back.

The top of the bag opened neatly, and the two U.N.C.L.E. agents bent over it together.

"Look at the wiring. Shoddy," said Illya. "Simply shoddy."

Napoleon reached in and lifted out a block of something brownish. "Here's the charge. Looks like plastique of some kind." He reached in with his other hand and produced a small complex device. "And here's the detonator. Let's save them. They might come in handy."

"If they'd work when we needed them," said Illya. "The explosive looks all right, but the detonator mechanism seems to have some loose parts."

Napoleon shrugged. "We can always rig up a detonator of our own," he said. "And you never know when you may need a few pounds of high explosive." He tossed it idly from hand to hand while Illya continued to rummage about in the bag, muttering to himself.

Finally, with a soft grunt of surprise, he brought out a set of batteries and held them out for Napoleon to see. They were standard squarish 9-volt cells, but they were yellow, and the inscription on the sides was in Arabic.

Napoleon looked down at them, quite puzzled, and finally took them from his partner's hand. He held them up and examined them closely. Then he looked at Illya. "Egyptian?" he said, doubtfully.

Illya nodded. "Apparently. And that plastique is the type the French were using in Algeria just a few years ago. I would call it fairly likely that this bomb was sent by someone with a base in Egypt. I wouldn't be too surprised if it turned out to be an official operation of Egyptian Intelligence, in fact."

This time Suzie looked puzzled too. "Egyptian? But that couldn't have been *their* rocket, could it?"

"Not likely," said Illya.

"Especially," added Napoleon, "if this is a sample of their technology. I've seen more care go into the construction of a Molotov cocktail than this shows. I wouldn't trust whoever built this to fire a skyrocket."

Illya glanced sideways at him. "Don't belittle our opponents just because they failed once, Napoleon. There is more than enough high explosive there to damage this corner of the hotel severely, not to mention its inhabitants, and it *could* have gone off. Remember, contempt breeds carelessness."

"But Egyptian?" Suzie asked again. "How? And why? And for that matter . . ."

"I'm sure we will find out eventually, Miss Danz," said Illya. "Our assignment, in fact, insists upon it. But first we must find Kurt Schneider."

"And to do that," said Napoleon, "we will have to start by finding Alexei Kropotkin and Archie Gunderson. Suzie, you have all those pictures you took during your adventure in the lifeboat—let's get some enlargements made of the shots you consider to be most recognizable of both of them. And we may as well get one of Kurt while we're about it."

"The slides should be back tomorrow," she said. "I sent them to the Kodak lab up in Johannesburg."

"Okay. We can save you some money and have the local U.N.C.L.E. darkroom run up enlargements for us. It would have been safer, by the way, if you'd given us the film to process. An accident at the lab could have been arranged."

"If the situation ever arises again, I'll be sure to remember," she said with a trace of irony in her voice.

"You do that," said Napoleon.

"Not to change the subject," said Illya, "but when we get the pictures, what do we do?"

"Time, as they so often say, is of the essence. You will head for the gay night life and sinful waterfront of Rio de Janiero and look for your compatriot, Kropotkin. I will brave the teeming streets of Victoria in a search for a Swedish seaman named Gunderson. Suzie will wait here where it is safe, and . . ."

"I shall do no such thing," said Suzie stubbornly. "The last thing Mac told me was to stay with you and help you. Archie is smart, and suspicious. He knows he's being looked for by people interested in killing him, and he wouldn't talk to you. But he'll remember me, and if I say you're all right, he'll coöperate."

She turned to Illya. "Alexei will probably be easier to approach. In the boat he kept talking about how lonely he was for Russia—all you'll have to do is speak to him and he'll be so happy he'll talk all night."

"But first I have to find him."

Napoleon shrugged. "That shouldn't be difficult. After all, how many Russian sailors can there be in a port the size of Rio de Janiero?"

"You would be surprised."

"Well, I'll bet there are a lot more Swedish ones in Hong Kong."

"But you'll have me helping you look," said Suzie.

Napoleon stopped and looked her over consideringly. "You know," he said, "that will just about make up for it."

She smiled.

Chapter 4

"You Know A Party Named Kropotkin?"

THE WATERFRONT AREA of Rio de Janiero is not the sort of place chosen for portrayal in travel folders. For one thing, it smells. A tourist guide could conceivably describe the concatenation of odors encountered there as "exotic," but the tourist would do well to remember that this word is also applied to inedible foods and loathsome jungle diseases. To Illya, whose nose was fairly cosmopolitan, the place simply stank.

A few blocks away, black oily water lapped at corroding pilings and tenders bobbed quietly under night-shrouded piers. Here, a few figures moved in the streets, reeling between islands of noise and light. Illya reeled among them, the better to avoid attention.

But a man alone always gets some attention. A soft voice came from a shadowed doorway: "Hey, sailor."

He turned and saw a figure in black. She stepped out, and a street-light half a block away shone off her leather vest and tight pants. She held an unlit cigarette. "Got a match?"

He looked her up and down and smiled thinly. She was better looking than most—she should have been working a better part of town. Unless she was working something other than the obvious, such as bait for a mugging gang. He fished in his pocket, every sense alert for a possible attack from behind. It hadn't come by the time his lighter was out.

The flame lit her face dramatically. Her hair was long and as black as the rest of her costume; her eyes were bright and sensuous. She let the smoke trickle from between her lips in irregular puffs as she spoke. "My name is Yanara. You are looking for a girl, maybe?"

"Not right now," said Illya. "I've got to find a man first. I owe him some money. He's a Russian sailor, off the *Duke of York*. If I can find him, maybe I'll have time for you."

"*Duke of York*? Came in just today. Hey, sailor, I'll wait for you. All men from *Duke of York* go to *A Fonte Sujo*. Captain is friend of owner, all crew go for drinking. You find your friend there, I bet. Then you come back?"

Illya nodded, but privately he doubted whether U.N.C.L.E. would authorize this item on his expense account. "Where is it?" he asked her.

A Fonte Sujo was readily identifiable by one of the few real illuminated signs in the area. A pattern of green lights, rather patchily outlining something like a fountain, flashed on and off in front of it, and the sounds of music and celebration made their way past the swinging doors.

Inside, the atmosphere was compounded of smoke, sweat and profanity. Illya stood with his back to the door, squinting through the gray-blue haze, until he saw a sailor not too drunk to walk approaching the bar. He moved forward and arrived alongside him.

"Hello, mate," he said. "You off the *Duke of York?*"

The other's eyes tracked, centered, and focused. "Yeah —why not?"

"Lemme buy you a drink."

The slack mouth curled up at the corners. "Sure—why not?"

Raw liquor splashed into dirty glasses, and a wordless toast was raised and drunk. Without wasting time, Illya got to business.

"You know a party named Kropotkin? He was on your ship this run."

"Kropotkin? I wouldn't call'm a party—'s more like a street fight. Friend of yours?"

"I owe him some money, and I'd better pay him before I spend it all."

The sailor laughed, choked, and needed another glass of whiskey. "He was around here just a a while ago— I saw him in the head. If he ain't shill here . . . *still* here . . . he's prob'ly gone back to the *Duke.*"

"Thanks, mate. I'll look around here."

"Hey, how 'bout another drink with your pal before you go?"

"Sure," said Illya. "Why not?"

The photographs of the Russian sailor firmly in his mind, Illya wandered among the tables, staggering slightly, following an apparently random pattern which nevertheless took him near every man in the place. He wound up at the back, where a small partition separated a few tables from the rest of the floor. Alone at one of them, his back to the wall, his eyes roving suspiciously about him, sat his quarry.

Illya approached him slowly, and waited for the eyes to focus on him. The man was not drunk; he was alert, and obviously on the edge of nervousness. Illya held out a hand to him. *"Zdrastvoutye, tovarich Kropotkin."*

"Who are you?" came the answer, also in Russian.

"Illya Nickovitch Kuryakin. MacKendricks sent me."

"MacKendricks is dead. Somebody killed him for what he saw. But I saw nothing. Go away."

"Waleed al-Fadly saw nothing also, but he was killed even before MacKendricks."

"What do you want with me? I know nothing. Go away."

"I want to talk to you about Kurt Schneider. The people who killed Mac are after him, and we have to find him before they do."

"Who are you?"

"Have you ever heard of the U.N.C.L.E.?"

"*Nyet.*"

One of the problems of being a secret organization, thought Illya, and said, "Then it would take too long to explain. But we can protect Kurt, and we must get some information from him."

"What kind of information? No, don't tell me. I don't want to know anything. Go away."

Illya shrugged and rose. Either a less direct or a more direct approach to interrogation was called for, and the bar was no place for either. Under the circumstances, he decided to wait and see which opportunity fate offered first.

He faded into the haze, and took a table where he could watch the door.

It was almost an hour later when Alexei Kropotkin stumbled through the crowd towards the exit. Two other men were reeling along with him, a total of six legs seeming scarcely enough to support and balance them all. Illya felt a twinge of frustration. Kropotkin backed up by two shipmates would be even less likely to feel coöperative, even if he was still sober enough to talk straight—which seemed doubtful.

Then Illya wondered carefully. Kropotkin had been rather pointedly alone before, and he didn't look like the type to become suddenly sociable. And he had been nursing a solitary beer. All things considered . . .

Illya stood up with studied unsteadiness, dropped some coins on the table and wandered towards the door.

Outside, fog was coming up from the harbor, and the air was warm and sticky. Illya hurried in the direction the three men had turned, trotting on silent rubber-soled feet. Ahead he could hear the clatter of incautious footsteps on the pavement.

It was late, and the streets were almost deserted. Here and there couples hurried to their various destinations, and occasional solitary figures reeled from doorway to doorway or strode purposefully on unguessable errands. But somewhere ahead, seen dimly through the floating veils of white, two men supporting a third hurried more than drunks would have been expected to. And Illya came behind them, but faster.

Then the street was empty, and the trio stopped. Illya faded into a shadow just as one of them turned around for a check of the vicinity. A light from somewhere caught an unexpected glitter in the other's hand. Illya propelled himself from hiding, feet pounding across the twenty-odd feet that separated him from the group.

His sudden appearance caught the two men by surprise, and they dropped their burden. One flashing hand struck the wrist of the knife-wielder, and the blade spun away into the dark. The other was reaching for his own weapon, but a soft shoe caught him in the pit of the stomach and he did a passable imitation of the knife.

The first man fell back a few steps, tugging at his pocket. Illya stepped forward and took his wrist in a bone-aching grip. "Don't you know it's dangerous to play with knives?" he inquired politely. "Sometimes they slip, and you get cut yourself."

He twisted at the wrist he held, pulling it out of the pocket, and another knife clattered to the stones. An application of pressure and a foot behind the other's ankles brought him to his knees with a gasp. "*Quem mandou você?*" he asked. "Who sent you?"

Shifting his grip to his left hand, he fumbled briefly

for the dropped knife. He brought it up slowly, level with the other's eyes. "Somebody paid you to get this particular sailor," he said softly. "Who was it?"

His subject's mouth remained stubbornly closed, but his eyes were very wide and focused on the point of the knife as it moved slowly back and forth like the swaying head of a coiled cobra.

"Would you have trouble breathing with your nose split?" asked Illya gently. "Or I could put your eyes out—very slowly. But I wouldn't do that until last." He touched the tip of the blade very lightly to the man's cheek and began to press. "It will be harder to talk when both your cheeks have been opened."

"No—no! I don't know who he was. A man with dark skin—like an *Indio* he was. But a strange accent. He paid us good money, and gave us a picture of the man, and his name—a funny name. He just said to take him out and kill him, and make it look like an ordinary street killing. There are many of them."

Illya considered this. "Where did he find you?"

"We met in Tiradentes Square. He told some people he needed a job done, and we were the cheapest who applied. It was all cash in advance."

"And you went ahead with the job after having been paid?"

"But of course, *senhor*," said the man, with a trace of injured pride in his voice. "Raul and I are honest men."

Slowly Illya let the knife down. The story was simple enough to be true, and nothing could be done about it. Tiradentes Square was the most likely spot in Brazil to find bargain-priced murderers, and every agent in the western hemisphere knew it. These scum probably deserved to die the same kind of death they had intended for Kropotkin, but in their world it would come for them soon enough, and unnecessary death was neither his specialty nor part of his assignment. He released the man's wrists and stepped back.

"All right. You've earned your money. Now get out of

here and take your brother with you. He'll feel better in a couple of days."

The man got slowly to his feet, and spoke hesitantly. "Uh, *senhor* . . . My knife?"

"What?"

"You have my knife."

Illya looked at him, wondering if he understood the implication. "That's right."

"Uh, I would like to have it back. It cost much money. It is a good knife." He gathered a little courage, and held out a hand. "*Senhor*, my wife would be very angry if I came home without it. She would think I sold it for wine. And I need it—to earn my living with."

Illya stared at the unsuccessful assassin, and shook his head slowly. "You'd better get started before I give you back your knife point first. I don't like you."

"But *senhor*—you don't know my wife . . ."

Illya took a menacing step towards him, and he fell back a pace. "Can you leave it in the alley after we go? I could come back for it later."

"Go!" shouted Illya angrily, as he felt the beginnings of sympathy rising for this amazingly inept little man, and unwilling to show him any more mercy than absolutely necessary.

Raul was still moving, down on the pavement some distance away, clutching spasmodically and gasping painfully. The knife-owner helped him to his feet and supported him as they started away. After a few steps he turned once more to say, "You could just toss it back in the alley . . ."

Illya cocked his arm to a throwing position, and the two scuttled away into the darkness.

Bright Brazilian sunlight poured golden across the sofa in the suite at the Leme Palace Hotel, where Illya had brought Alexei Kropotkin the night before. The sailor, with administrations of coffee and thiamine pills, had recovered nicely from the aftereffects of the chloral hydrate he had ingested along with his last beer.

His two would-be killers had also been impatient to get the job over with, and had taken him along while he was still conscious, but unable to control his movements.

He nodded in agreement with Illya's comment on his luck. "With two *balvani* like that, they could as easily have given me too much rather than too little. And then they wouldn't have needed the knives."

"Did you understand what they were saying?"

"I could hear them, but I don't know the language. This Portuguese is beyond me except for a few necessary words like *cerveja* and *puta,* and they didn't get mentioned."

Illya had spent most of an hour convincing Alexei of the facts as far as they were known. He even went so far as to tell him about the bomb in his baggage in Capetown, though not so far as to tell him where Napoleon and Suzie had gone. He started to explain about the rocket, but Kropotkin stopped him again. "*Nyet.* I do not understand, so do not tell me. The less I know of it the happier I shall be."

"But you do know something," said Illya. "Kurt Schneider talked to you before you all split up in Capetown. Mac had implied there might be trouble about what you had seen . . ."

"I saw nothing! *Nitchevo!*"

"You saw the *Paxton Merchant* being blown up by a guided missile, and that is enough. But we must find Kurt Schneider. With MacKendricks dead, he is the only man left who knows where that island is. He must have told you something."

Kropotkin lay back on the couch, his forearms over his eyes. "We were talking about going our various ways, that last night. We had dinner, all six of us, and after Mac took Suzie back to the hotel, the rest of us went to . . . well, someplace else for a celebration. We'd been at sea a long time," he said in faint apology, and continued. "There was some trouble at first—they wouldn't let Waleed in on account of his skin, but Kurt and Archie and I told them he was as white a man as ever walked through their dirty doors, and offered to take the whole place apart for them if they tried to keep him out, and they talked it over for a minute and sort of saw it our way." He smiled in memory, and then his face clouded over suddenly. "And then somebody killed him, just like they tried to kill me last night!" He pounded a great fist on the upholstered arm of the sofa, and swore bitterly in Russian. "*Svolochi!* He was a nice little guy. They didn't have no call to kill him."

"What did Kurt say about hiding?" Illya asked, after several seconds of silence.

"Nothing. Archie wanted to know, so we could sort of keep in touch. But Kurt just said he was going down in something. He and Archie spoke German between themselves, mostly, but English with me. He and Archie got to be good friends. Kurt missed Germany as much as I miss Byelorussia, and Archie knew his country well. They would talk for hours about it—I had no one to talk to about my homeland. Then they would remember me, and apologize. But all Kurt ever told me was that he would be hiding under something, I think, maybe like digging a hole down under a rock. That was what he said—he'd be going down under something."

"Was that all?"

"I'm afraid so. I owe you a great debt, Illya, and I cannot pay it properly without information—but I have given you all I have."

Illya shrugged and rose to his feet. "You'd better stay hidden for a while," he said. "Whoever is behind this is not likely to stop until he's sure you're safely out of the way. Do you have someplace to go?"

Kropotkin nodded. "There is a place on the *Santa Rosalia*, sailing from Buenos Aires in five days. I can get my gear from the *Duke* today; these mysterious people will think I am dead for a while anyway when I am not on the ship. And then I shall go under another name. I can get across the border—I have friends in Uruguay—and then I shall disappear. But where can I see you again, my friend? After all, for saving my life I should at least buy you a drink."

"Look me up if you ever dock in New York," said Illya.

"New York?" Kropotkin smiled widely. "And are there good Russian restaurants there? I miss the food of my home very much."

Illya nodded. "Very good ones. But you may be in danger there for some time. I suggest you stay in hiding for several months, and enjoy the foreign food. You would not enjoy the finest piroshki if you swallowed them with a cut throat."

Kropotkin slapped himself on the chest. "I can take care of myself."

"Perhaps. But stay out of dark alleys, and don't drink with strangers—even Russians."

Section II : "They Built Themselves A Monster Wheel . . ."

Chapter 5

"Neu-Schloss? Where's That?"

TWO DAYS BEFORE Illya Kuryakin fought in a hot, fog-filled alley in Rio de Janiero, a quarter of the way around the world a young man in a white coat had looked up from a tracking telescope and called to an older man. The strange tone in his voice brought his superior at once.

"Doctor—here's the source of those signals. It matches the radar trace."

"Well, what is it?"

"Uh . . . I'd rather you looked yourself, sir, before I describe what it looks like to me."

The old man bent to the eyepiece and touched the focusing control. He stayed there for several seconds, then finally spoke without removing his eye from the telescope. "It looks like a wheel—a monstrous wheel. Turning slowly about a central hub. I can see a pair of opposed spokes. Hmm. It could well be two hundred feet across, as the radar scan indicated."

"But, Doctor—what is it doing there?"

After several seconds the answer came, distant and distracted. "A good question. A very good question. And one which, in a few days, the world may well be asking. What *is* it doing there?"

It was actually four days before photographs and official statements were released to the press of the world —or as much of the world as had a press that could demand such things. The photographs were blurred and grainy, demonstrating the scientific fact of atmospheric interference with serious attempts at astronomical photography, but revealing very little about the thing they called the "Monster Wheel." The statements varied between "No Comment" and "Steps Are Being Taken," neither of which were any more satisfying than the photographs. Flying saucer societies hailed the impending arrival of delegations from their favorite planets. Military men in all parts of the world chewed their nails, and talked to themselves late into the night. "It's got to be Theirs, but why haven't They announced it? And if it's ours, why haven't *we* announced it, and why haven't they told *me*? I'm important—I have a *right* to know these things." The public glanced over their shoulders shortly after sunset, saw a bright fast-moving star, and said, if they noticed it, "Huh! Another satellite. Big one, looks like." And the Monster Wheel said nothing, but twittered and hummed and buzzed on a couple of very high radio frequencies. Nothing could be made of the telemetered signals.

And in the city of Kowloon, across Victoria Harbour from Hong Kong, Napoleon Solo and Suzie Danz were occupied with the search for a missing sailor.

They had arrived at Kai Tak airport the same day the *Miyako Maru* tied up at the Whampoa docks, and had been there to meet her. The crew would be given no shore liberty until the task of unloading had been completed, but patience was a virtue Napoleon was cultivating. Unobtrusively, he and Suzie had taken a place near the forward gangplank to scan the faces of the workers on the deck, and to watch them as they left the ship as evening drew on.

At length the line of men checked out with the first mate at the head of the gangway and the last of them hurried to solid land in search of whatever shore leave held for him. Suzie turned to Napoleon, with a puzzled expression. "Are you sure this was the right ship?"

Napoleon looked up at the nearest life preserver and read off the characters on it. "*Miyako Maru.* That's what U.N.C.L.E. intelligence told us. "Let's make polite inquiries aboard."

He swung up the ramp and greeted the mate with the clipboard politely. "We're looking for a friend of mine named Archie Gunderson. Has he gone ashore yet?"

The mate looked at him suspiciously, and then at his list. "Yah. He go ashore mebbe ten, fifteen minutes ago."

Napoleon registered disappointment. "I don't suppose he mentioned where he'd be going?"

"Nah. Dey get der pay, dey go ashore. Mebbe dey come back, mebbe dey don't. How come you want him?"

"Well, like I said—I'm an old friend of his. We were on the . . ah . . . the *Nancy Brig* together ten years ago."

"You don' look like you ever work freight."

"Well, it's been a long time. Look here," he went on, producing a thousand-yen note, "I'd sure appreciate it if you could find out where he went, or when he'd be back."

The mate looked at the money without a change of his sour expression. "I tell you he gone—he gone. You want a lie for your money?"

Napoleon considered this, then reluctantly folded the note back into its hiding place. "Ah . . . no. But if you see him . . ."

"I tell him you look for him."

"No, don't do that either. I want to surprise him. After all, he hasn't seen me for quite a while." He added a laugh that sounded foolish even to himself, and started down the ramp again. The mate looked after him, then shook his head slightly and returned to the manifests.

He shrugged at Suzie. "He must have gotten past us. The Keeper of the Way up there says he went ashore ten or fifteen minutes ago."

"But I didn't see him. And I *would* have recognized him."

"Maybe he's grown a beard."

"He grew one while we were in the lifeboat. Not a big one, but I know how he'd look. Napoleon," she said, "either he's still on that ship or he left as soon as she docked and that man is trying to protect him. Or maybe" —her voice dropped—"maybe that man killed him and threw the body overboard, and now he'll try to prove he actually went ashore and will never be seen again!" She looked up the side of the ship suspiciously to the thin figure that leaned on the railing, silhouetted against the early evening sky, still working over his clipboard. "I think we should go up there and make sure."

"How?"

"Well—ask him, I guess."

"And hope he reveals something out of surprise?"

"It works in the detective stories—and anyway, you can threaten him."

"Look, Suzie—we're in a foreign country. If U.N.C.L.E. wasn't pretty highly regarded, I wouldn't be able to carry this gun at all. The government wouldn't like it if I started waving it around to impress people. Besides, it's bad form."

She clenched her little fists and made a face. "All right then, you wait here! I'll go up there and see what I can scare out of him!"

And she stamped to the gangplank and started up. Napoleon was right behind her—after all, he had a responsibility here too.

Suzie stepped past the railing and began fiercely without even waiting for the man to look up. He did soon enough.

"Now look here," she said. "It's very important that we find Archie Gunderson as soon as possible. I know he didn't leave this ship in the last two hours. Now where is he, and what have you done with him?"

The mate lifted his head, looked her over slowly and carefully, and said nothing. His eyes flicked briefly over her shoulder, then returned to his work, ignoring her protest.

Napoleon had caught the glance, and looked down at his wristwatch. The silver case had a large enough flat area to serve as an unobtrusive mirror, and he twisted his wrist slightly, scanning the deck behind them. There was a figure in the door to the wheelhouse. It was too dark to see clearly, but it seemed to be holding something.

The U.N.C.L.E. agent didn't lower his arm but let it slip inside his coat. While the little automatic shouldn't be waved about casually, it wasn't there just to compliment the color scheme of his ensemble.

A soft, deep voice from behind him stopped his hand just as his fingers closed around the butt.

"Don't try it mister. I ain't a very fast shot, but it'd take you a while to turn around."

Suzie whirled around at once, and Napoleon instinctively grabbed for his gun, expecting a repeat of her incisive action in Capetown. The automatic was halfway out and he was on one knee facing the big blond-bearded man in the doorway as Suzie cried, "Archie! Don't shoot him!"

She didn't specify whom she was addressing, but both men heeded her suggestion, probably fortunately for both of them.

Archie frowned doubtfully, not lowering his .45. "Is he okay, Miss Suzie?"

"Oh yes! He's from U.N.C.L.E., and he saved my life when they killed Mac! Did you know about that? You must have."

The big man nodded, and the gun muzzle drooped slowly. "When I heard about Mac and Waleed, I t'ought somet'ing big was wrong, and I t'ought I'd be ready if it came after me. And when I see you with this man, I t'ink maybe they make you find me."

"Archie! You don't think I'd do something like that!"

He lifted his shoulders slightly. "They can get pretty bad to a girl, Miss Suzie. That's why I was ready to kill him."

Napoleon rose awkwardly to his feet, restored his U.N.-C.L.E. Special to its accustomed place, and brushed at his clothes. "Well, I'm glad you didn't have to." He stuck out a hand, half expecting a bone-crushing grip. "My name is Napoleon Solo."

Gunderson shifted the automatic to his left hand and shook. The grip was firm, but not powerful. The man knew how to use his strength, which would make him doubly dangerous in a fight. His blue eyes were cool, and alert. "U.N.C.L.E.?" he said. "I t'ink I remember Mac talking about it one time, two-three years ago. And if Suzie likes you, I'm satisfied."

He remembered the automatic in his left hand and tucked it back in the waistband of his trousers, then called across to the first mate, who had stood unmoved, even during the imminent shooting match: "Okay, Fish-eye. Signal if somebody else comes looking around the ship. We'll be in the wheelhouse for a little while."

Then they were seated around a small table. Gunderson was interested in the circumstances of Mac's death, and clapped Suzie proudly on the shoulder when Napoleon told of her part in the battle. He could offer no possible explanation for the interest of Egyptian agents, unless that country had a secret missile capability. "I don't think they have," he rumbled. "But it is true that a lot of Germans went to Egypt when the War ended." Napoleon noticed his Scandinavian accent seemed to lessen as he talked with them, and made a mental note to keep an eye on this man who seemed, on examination, to be rather more than the simple sailor he appeared on the surface.

"Possibly they were hired by another country," Solo suggested. "But the question remains as to just what island you saw the missile fired from. Aerial reconnaissance of the whole area has found many tiny volcanic islands, none of which show any signs of being a missile launching site. And as I'm sure you know, it takes quite a bit of hardware on the ground to get a modern missile into space."

Archie nodded. "And this is why you have to find Kurt. Well, all I can tell you isn't very much. Kurt and Alexei and Waleed and I had a sort of celebration in Capetown the night before we were to sail—no, after you and Mac left, Miss Suzie. We were . . . well, we were sailors out for a last night on the town, and it wasn't the sort of thing you could have come along for. We all said where we were going from Capetown, and Kurt didn't want to say at first. But I think there might be trouble after us, so I keep after him. And finally he got a little drunk, and whispered the name of the place. *Neu-Schloss,* he said. And I remember it. *Neu-Schloss.*"

Napoleon leaned back with a sigh and a smile of satisfaction. They had their goal in sight at last. He thought a minute, and frowned. "*Neu-Schloss?* Where's that?"

The sailor smiled a little and stood up. "I start wondering that myself when I hear about Mac being murdered." He pulled down a large book from the shelf and latched the door again. "Take a look in the gazetteer."

Napoleon accepted the book, opened to the middle and started flipping through the N's. "Neurara, Neuruppin, Neuse River," he said. "Neuss, Neustadt. . . . There are certainly enough Neustadts. . . . Neustrelitz, Neu-Ulm, Neuville, Neuwarp, Neuwied . . ." He stopped and ran his finger back up the column. "Hm."

"I check the other atlases here. There is no such listing."

"Could he have been making a joke?" Suzie asked.

Gunderson shook his massive head. "I don't think so. He seem very serious about it. He tell me because he say I am smarter than the other two, and if there is trouble he trust me to know what to do. But he was pretty drunk, I guess."

Napoleon saw his trail evaporating like a mirage. He closed the book with a deep and heartfelt sigh. "This will take some thought," he said. "Some heavy thought.

And possibly even some detective work." He leaned back in the chair and thought until Suzie interrupted him.

"Have you thought of anything?"

He straightened up. "As a matter of fact I have. It's getting rather late, and I don't recall having eaten for several hours."

She nodded. "That's worth thinking about."

"That's even worth doing something about. Why don't the three of us go for dinner someplace?"

"Marvelous," said Suzie, without a trace of sarcasm in her tone. "Do you know a good place?"

"I seem to remember a good restaurant at the corner of Mongkok Road and Reclamation Street."

"The *Yen Chi*," said Archie unexpectedly. "A good place."

Napoleon shrugged. "If you like Chinese food."

Chapter 6

"I'll Show You A Magic Trick."

DINNER WAS excellent. Suzie was at least enough of a world traveler not to ask what she was eating, and in fact was able to recognize most of it. The meal was leisurely and enjoyable, but Archie grew uneasy as the hour grew later, and pointed out that wandering the streets of Kowloon after dark was asking for trouble, with unknown powers almost certainly after them. Over drinks, Napoleon and Suzie were discussing the situation.

"It's early morning in New York, and a couple hours later in Rio, if Illya's still there. When we get to the hotel, I'll check in and see what results our South American department has had in this investigation. I hope he had better luck than we did."

"And if he didn't?"

"We all go home and wait for our international network of eyes and ears to send word on Schneider. You can find a needle in the biggest haystack if you have enough people looking, for long enough."

"But how long do we have?"

Napoleon took a drink from his iced glass and rolled it around in his mouth a while before swallowing and answering. "We don't even know what's going on on that island. The rocket you saw launched obviously wasn't an attack on anybody—*that* we would have heard about. It might have put something small into orbit; anything big would certainly have been spotted. There are a surprising number of people all over the world who are paid to do nothing but stare at the sky and take notes on anything that moves. Or it could have been a test. It may have failed; it may have succeeded. If it succeeded, they may be very close to doing . . . whatever it is they want to do. If it failed, they may still be very close. Or they may not. The only way to find out without finding them first is to wait until they either announce themselves, or they succeed. And then it will probably be too late to stop them, if indeed they even should be stopped."

"Who decides whether they should?" asked Archie.

"Not me. And in something as big as this could be, not my superior either. There's someone—several someones, for all I know—over him. This business could be big enough to plunge the whole world into atomic war in a matter of hours if something went wrong."

Suzie shuddered and finished her drink quickly. "Let's hope nothing goes wrong, then."

Napoleon nodded. "*That's* my department. And since it is getting fairly late, I think I should keep our own exposure to danger to a minimum. I'll get a taxi to run us down to the hotel, and drop Archie off at the *Miyako Maru* on the way."

Service was prompt for the late hour, and a taxi appeared less than five minutes after the call. They loaded in, and Solo gave the driver directions to the Whampoa docks. The man nodded, and the little car leaped off up Mongkok Road. Three blocks later it turned left on Nathan, away from the downtown and the docks. Napoleon leaned forward.

"The Whampoa docks, driver," he said. "You should have turned right. Take the next right."

The driver released a flood of Chinese in an inland dialect Napoleon couldn't follow. He attempted Cantonese, and got no answer.

During the time this took, the taxi had crossed Boundary and started up a grade. The clapboard shanties became smaller and even less attractive, and there were fewer people on the road. Here and there a cultivated patch showed between the hovels, and only the tiny cooking fires marked the edges of the road.

Napoleon leaned back. "Something's wrong," he muttered to his friends, as he slipped his automatic out of its spring-clip holster. "We're going the wrong way."

A sign flashed by, flaring briefly in the headlights: TAI PO ROAD. An arrow bore to the right, and the car followed it.

Napoleon leaned forward again and said quietly, "You understood English well enough when we got in. Now understand this. Either you stop and turn this car around, or you'll see your brains splattered over the inside of the windshield."

The car slowed as the driver reached for the dashboard and pulled a knob. There was a *pwangg!* of a strong spring released and a sheet of metal shot up from the back of the front seat. It caught Napoleon across the wrist, a numbing blow that knocked the gun from his hand and almost cracked the bone. The gun fell into the front seat as the shield thumped against the roof, and Napoleon fell back.

Suzie leaned over him. "Napoleon!" she said. "What's going on?"

"Well, I wouldn't like to jump to an unwarranted conclusion, but I think we're being kidnapped." He picked himself up to a proper sitting position, massaging his wrist gingerly.

"But where could they be taking us?"

Archie scowled. "British possession is not very big. The only other place they could go is over the border."

"And that," said Napoleon, "is what I expect will happen."

Suzie looked shocked. "But I can't go over the border! I don't have a visa for Red China!"

"None of us do," said Napoleon. "That makes it a good place to get rid of us. But we have some twenty miles to go yet, if I remember this road, and I expect a helicopter from downtown can pull us out of the fire long before we get there." He winced slightly as he bent his wrist towards an inside pocket and pulled out his transceiver.

"Channel L, please. Channel L." The only answer was a burst of static.

He adjusted something slightly, pulled up the tiny antenna, and called again. Only the hiss and roar of a jammed frequency answered him. He sighed and replaced the device. "Well," he said, "it looks as if we'll have to get ourselves out of this one."

Some twenty minutes later the taxi pulled off the road and bumped to a stop near a cluster of huts surrounded by angular terraced hills. Shadowy figures hurried out of one of the huts as the taxi flashed its lights. They opened the doors from the outside, and regarded the three sleepers in the back seat for a moment. Then a quiet command in Chinese, and the three were picked up and borne back into the building.

The fresh air began to revive them, and Napoleon gradually became aware of being supported by his knees and armpits. Then a door slammed somewhere beyond his head, and he was put down on his back on a rough floor. A voice in accented English said, "They are coming around. You didn't use enough gas after all."

Napoleon thought, *As long as they know, there's not much use pretending.* He groaned a little and tried to sit up. Then he groaned realistically. Whatever they had used on him had left quite a headache. He forced open an eye and tried to bring the room into focus. It almost worked.

By the light of a single swinging lightbulb, five armed men were directing their attention towards the three figures on the floor. Archie was already sitting up, breathing deeply and looking around. Suzie was just beginning to move.

One of the men spoke. "Before you stand up, Mr. Solo, please to empty out your pockets completely. You, also, Mr. Gunderson."

Napoleon slowly went through his various pockets, laying out an assortment of things. One of the five came forward and took them. He nodded at the "fountain pen" and the cigarette case-lighter, and set them aside. The other objects he dropped into a small plastic bag of the type morgues use to contain the effects of the deceased. Napoleon noted the similarity, and carefully refrained from thinking about it.

The last item to be brought out was the Gyrojet pistol, which had been resting lightly in a deep-cut inside pocket of his coat. Its few ounces did not bag the jacket, and it was conveniently located. The Chinese lifted his gun warningly as Napoleon brought it out, and held out his other hand.

He took the little pistol, hefted it, and looked at it carefully. Then he held it up contemptuously for the others to see. "The American carries another gun! A toy one to frighten us with!"

The tall thin one who seemed to be the leader came forward and examined it closely. "Why do you carry a toy gun, Mr. Solo?"

Napoleon looked a little embarrassed. "Well," he said,

"I just picked it up this afternoon for my nephew. He likes magic tricks."

"This is a trick gun? It does not just go *click-click?*"

"Well, not exactly. It's really sort of remarkable. A tribute to the ingenuity of your toymakers, and a whole lot of fun, too."

"What does it do?" The Chinese was beginning to be interested. Obviously this little contraption of stamped tin could not be a danger against five armed men, but he was still uncertain as to what it really was. "In my experience agents of the U.N.C.L.E. do not carry toy guns without reason."

Napoleon shrugged. "I would have left it at my hotel if we'd been there since I bought it."

The tall man suddenly pointed the pistol at Napoleon and pulled the trigger. Nothing happened. And Napoleon, who knew better than to carry a gun cocked with a round in the chamber, didn't even flinch. Instead he laughed easily. "Not like that," he said condescendingly. "Here. Let me show you." He held out his hand casually.

The other stepped back quickly. "No—you tell me how it works," he said, but his tone was doubtful. It felt so much like a harmless toy, and perhaps it would be amusing. . . .

Napoleon looked patient. "It's very difficult to explain without showing you on the gun what I am talking about. It took the clerk at the toy store fifteen minutes to teach me how to work it properly."

The Chinese thought, and looked around a moment at the other two prisoners for clues. Suzie was staring in complete puzzlement, and Archie was watching impatiently, tapping his fingers on the floor where he sat. It seemed an insane waste of time to be playing with a toy gun when their lives were at stake.

At last he reached a decision. He handed the gun to Napoleon, saying, "All right. But remember you are covered by several armed men, and there are more outside. And do not try anything foolish like a cyanide spray; I will stay well away from you." And he backed to the opposite wall.

Napoleon observed that only two men had their machine pistols at a ready position, and only one of them had the bolt cocked. He smiled inanely as he held up the pistol like a conjurer. "Now you see," he said foolishly, "I have here what appears to be an ordinary gun. Watch closely—I have nothing up my sleeves—and observe that during this entire performance my fingers will never leave my hands." He wiggled his fingers, and saw five pairs of eyes fixed fascinated on them.

He took the pistol in firing position in his right hand, and blew down the barrel. "Observe," he continued, "the barrel is completely empty."

"So's your head," muttered Gunderson, from the floor.

"Quiet, there," said Napoleon, aiming a mock kick at the sailor, and continuing his pitch. He had to have every bit of their attention on him and none on their machine guns if this magic trick was to succeed. Archie had just cost him some of it.

Improvising desperately, he continued: "This pistol was sold to me by a wise old gunsmith who had studied the ancient arts of the inscrutable East. Its operation is a secret known only to the adepts of a mysterious society and learned by me at the risk of my life. Now you will be among the privileged few who have seen with their own eyes the wonderful secret guarded for generations by devoted servants of ancient wisdom." That did it—only one muzzle still pointed at them, and the man behind it was completely fascinated by Napoleon's spiel.

"Watch closely, now. . . ." He brought up the Gyrojet. "I push forward this small lever on the side, made of silver from the deepest mines of Afghanistan. . . ." He pulled the cocking lever forward and down and put off the safety. He looked up at them, and his face wore a broad inane smile.

The smile remained fixed on his face as he centered the pistol on the first guard and pulled the trigger. He swung the gun slightly and fired again. Five shots tore across the room in four seconds. A slug ripped into the chest of the third man before the first hit the ground, and the last barely had his machine pistol up and cocked before it was too late for him to pull the trigger. Without a wisp of recoil to compensate for, only the slightest movement of the wrist was necessary to correct the aim, and the little missiles were accurate enough over twenty feet to kill dependably. Especially since the propellant continued to burn for a fraction of a second after they penetrated the body.

Napoelon Solo was still grinning foolishly as he slowly lowered the gun. There was a smell of burning, and a small amount of smoke in the little room, yet there had been comparatively little noise. But now there were five crumpled bodies against the far wall, and four fully loaded machine guns they would need no longer.

Suzie stared, her mouth open, her eyes tracking slowly from the "toy pistol" to the five bodies, and back again. Napoleon looked down at her, spread his arms slightly, and bowed from the waist.

"Hey, presto," he said softly.

"Napoleon," said Suzie, gradually recovering her voice. "What did you *do*?"

He smiled just a little, and canted his head towards the far wall. "Magic," he said. "I just made the entire world disappear—as far as they are concerned."

"It's a rocket pistol," said Archie, rising to his feet. "I saw an article on it in a magazine some time ago. Gun is just a tin launching tube with hammer and trigger. Bullet full of rocket fuel, supplies its own power. I recognize it from picture."

"Then why did you break their concentration on me?" asked Napoleon. "Didn't you think I knew what I was doing?"

"Yah, but the tall one was looking pretty edgy. I

t'ought I'd make him feel better for the few seconds he had left."

Solo had already retrieved his belongings, and was checking out the little silver transceiver. "Channel L, please. . . ."

And a voice answered, "Hong Kong office. Go ahead, please."

Everyone heaved a sigh of relief. "Agent Solo here. We've been kidnapped, but are now free of surveillance and jamming, and would like some help and transportation. No medical aid necessary, but come in prepared to defend yourselves. There may be more guards outside."

"Right-ho. We have a fix on your position—about halfway out on the Tai Po Road, a little north of Tai Po Tau. Helicopter should be there in ten or fifteen minutes. Now if you'll stand by, there is a call for you from New York. Switch over to Channel D, please."

There was a hum, and a couple of clicks, and Waverly's familiar gravelly voice came small and tinny from the tiny speaker. "Mr. Solo, what seems to be the trouble? You've been out of touch, and the area control reports our general frequency interfered with."

"Well, I've made contact with Gunderson, sir, and gotten what information he had. We'll have to discuss its evaluation in light of whatever Illya has come up with. But we were kidnapped this evening, and they wouldn't let us use the telephone."

"By agents of a certain North African power?"

"Ah—I don't think so, sir. Oddly enough, this whole operation seems quite different in style." He bent over one of the bodies, and picked up a machine pistol with his free hand. "In fact, I would say there were no hieroglyphics involved here at all."

"Interesting. Is there another nation striving to protect its secrets?"

"Not exactly, sir. This particular job has bird-tracks all over it." He looked down at the Schmeisser. The swaying yellow bulb overhead picked out in sharp black and white an image of a stylized bird in fighting posture blazoned on the short stock—a Thrush. "Perhaps this puts things in a new light."

There was a brief silence from New York. "Perhaps it does. Mr. Kuryakin regrets to announce contact made, but no information available. His transcript of the interrogation is under study now, and there may be some indication of direction after all. We shall discuss this later over a more secure communications channel."

"Very good, sir. I'll call you from Hong Kong. Solo out."

They remained inside the small building, keeping low, Archie and Napoleon with captured machine guns trained on the door. There was no sound from without, though, until some ten minutes later the racket of a helicopter faded softly in from the distance. Napoleon opened his transceiver again.

"Solo calling U.N.C.L.E. helicopter. There's been no activity around here. Either they're all gone, or they're hiding waiting for you. Knock before you come in—we have the door covered."

"Right-ho, Solo," said a distant voice. "We're scanning the area with the infrareds, right now. See no sign of life. They may have got the wind up and fled before us. Hope so, what?"

It appeared so. The helicopter landed without drawing a shot from cover, and the men who sprinted from it towards the small shack passed without comment. They straightened and looked around, then knocked.

"Who goes?" said Napoleon.

"Friends," said a voice, "with a machine to get the three of you back to town. You have a conversation to complete with New York."

"Come on in, then. It isn't locked."

In another minute they were all loaded into the helicopter, and the roar of the motor deepened as the blades bit into the air and lifted them away. The machine wheeled around, then leaned forward and thundered off over the night-darkened mountains, due south towards the island of Hong Kong.

Inside the cabin, Archie Gunderson was saying, "I t'ank you very much, Mr. Solo, but I t'ink I go hide by myself. After this, these people know me, and I better dig a hole someplace and pull it in after me. Don't worry, I let you know where I am. But don't worry—I been chased by experts."

"If that's the way you want it, Archie, okay. Just learn from tonight, and never take the first cab that offers itself."

"Yah, Mr. Solo—or the second."

Chapter 7

"Sing For Us, Rameses."

THE U.N.C.L.E. office in Hong Kong looked like U.N.C.L.E. offices all over the world. And the communications room, where Napoleon Solo sat before a microphone, was identical. His transmission was being effectively scrambled, as were the two voices that came through his earphones. It was three o'clock in the morning in Hong Kong, which made it the middle of the afternoon in New York and in Rio.

"Section Four bears out your initial findings, Mr. Solo—there is no city in the world named Neu-Schloss. It is possible that Schneider merely invented a name to satisfy his companions, suspecting the possible consequences of the destruction of the *Paxton Merchant* and wishing to cover as much of his trail as possible."

"Ah—with all due respect, sir, I don't think so. The four of them were friends, and trusted each other. Everyone seems to have a great respect for Schneider; not the sort you'd have for a man who would lie to you that casually."

Illya's voice said: "I tend to agree with Napoleon, sir. Add to this the fact that all of them had faced death together and lived in circumstances of extreme forced intimacy for some time. This sort of thing can build a tremendous mutual trust. I don't think it would be betrayed lightly."

"In that case, we can only assume he told the truth, and was in fact intending to go to . . . Neu-Schloss. If he did not intend to conceal his destination, he must have believed his friends would know where this was. Do they?"

Both agents were definite. Their informants sincerely believed they had imparted all the information they possessed to the U.N.C.L.E. agents.

"We have all the clues we're going to get," said Napoleon thoughtfully. "All that remains is to put them together."

"Admirable, Mr. Solo. Have you any suggestions as to how we might begin?"

"Didn't Kropotkin say that Schneider and Gunderson usually spoke German together? Neu-Schloss means New Castle in German."

"New Castle? There must be dozens of them," said Illya.

"There are a dozen or more in Europe alone," said Waverly. "In as many different languages. It would appear that when, in the middle ages, a nobleman chose to build a new castle, the nearest town would take its name from it."

"And do we have any indication as to which of all the New Castles in the world he meant?"

"Section Four has just offered a suggestion," Waverly said, "to the effect that the terms 'under' and 'down,' as used to Mr. Kropotkin, may refer to 'down under,' or Australia and New Zealand."

"There's a Newcastle in Australia, isn't there?"

"That is correct, Mr. Solo. A port city, as a matter of

fact, some hundred miles north of Sydney. A reasonable choice. Stand by, please."

There was a click, and Napoleon said tentatively, "Illya? Still there?"

"Yes. While we're waiting, you may as well tell me what you did wrong this evening."

"Don't tell me you've already heard about the—"

"The kidnapping? You should know how efficient Section Five is. I imagine the whole world knows by now—it's been several hours."

"I don't suppose you made any mistakes in Rio."

"None worth mentioning. Of course, I was up against a less formidable opponent. He didn't even do the job himself—hired a couple of local long-knives to fill in for him. They weren't quite up to it."

"Proving once again the essential folly of taking the lowest competitive bid."

There was another click, and Waverly's voice returned: "Section Four, with some help from their computer, reports that the *Odile* sailed from Capetown for Sydney the day after the *Duke of York*. It will be some hours before we can check her crew list for Kurt Schneider, but this is the most likely ship to have taken him to his 'Neu-Schloss.' The *Magdalene* sailed for Melbourne six days later, and will not have arrived yet. Both of you will proceed to Newcastle via Sydney, and begin the search for Schneider. If you have found no trace of him in three days, go to Melbourne and meet the *Magdalene*. Report back when you have something—positive or negative—to report."

"Not both of us, sir," corrected Napoleon politely. "All three."

All three of them sat around a table at a small sidewalk cafe in Newcastle, New South Wales. The hot yellow Australian sun splashed over the street and bright shards of it glittered back from the bay where the dredgers were black shadows as they worked endlessly to keep the harbor clear.

They had found the *Odile* the day before, and approached her master. When shown Suzie's photographs of Kurt, he had looked doubtful, and called to his First. They held a brief animated discussion in Greek, too fast and colloquial for Napoleon to follow.

Finally the Captain turned back to them. "*Tañta,*" he said. "Yes. Willie Muller. From Capetown. He left—went north on train."

"North?" said Illya. "Newcastle, of course."

That afternoon they had emulated him. And this day they had shown his picture to several dozen bartenders, hotel clerks and waitresses in the waterfront area without eliciting any response. They had reported both the positive and negative results to Waverly, and received only scant encouragement in return. The three men met again for an early supper to compare notes.

"Well," said Illya, "I must admit Newcastle's a friendly city, even if not an especially observant one. If we weren't morally certain he'd come here, I'd say we were on a wild German chase."

"Maybe we're limiting ourselves unnecessarily," said Napoleon thoughtfully. "We've been looking mostly around the waterfront area. Now, if I were a sailor on the run, I think I'd stay away from the waterfront; especially if I were as smart a man as Kurt."

"But if you were that smart," suggested Illya seriously, "you would expect your pursuers to think of that too, and you would go straight to the waterfront, knowing it would be the last place they'd look for you."

"But they're smart too," said Suzie. "They'd expect that."

"Right," said Napoleon. "Therefore I'd hide out uptown somewhere—as I just said."

"Oh."

"Of course."

They sat in silence for a few seconds.

"It would be easier if you knew more about him," said Illya suddenly. "Interests, possible diversions and entertainments he might seek. As it is, about all we know is that he's German."

Napoleon said something impolite under his breath and slapped the table top. "We're slipping, Illya. We really are slipping. Tomorrow morning we start the rounds of German restaurants, any Hofbraus we can locate in the telephone directory tonight. And tonight we check for any theaters showing German films. Remember him telling Kropotkin he was homesick? If we don't get a lead out of this tomorrow I'll eat a kangaroo." He thought a moment. "A small one, and roasted."

The estimate turned out to be pessimistic. Two theaters were running German films, and the boxoffice clerk at one recognized the picture of Schneider, as a man who had been there just the night before. She remembered him because he had left with one of their regular customers—an old German expatriate who came every week to the theater, but twice when a German film was on. No, she didn't know his name, but the manager might. . . .

He did, and after some convincing and a small bribe he was kind enough to share it with them. As they sought him out, Illya remarked to Suzie, "And so, once again, standard police procedure pays off. It's routine, boring, and time consuming, but it works."

"Inspiration helps," said Napoleon defensively.

Once they showed the old man their identification and told him some of the story, he was persuaded to recall his companion of the previous evening. He and Kurt had fallen into conversation between films, and had found out they were both from Stuttgart. The old man had left in 1935, accurately forseeing the destiny of the Third Reich, and had built a new life in Australia. But the pleasure of talking to someone who knew his home town had revived memories of his childhood, and he and Schneider had talked the night away.

"You will think me a self-centered old fool," he said, "but I am afraid I can remember little of what he said. We talked mostly about Germany when the Nazis came. He told me a little of how the War had changed it—and I did not want to hear more." He shook his head sadly. "I do not think now I will go back after all. It would not be my home anymore."

"But did he say anything about where he was going?" Illya asked.

The old man thought. "He only hinted. I asked him if we could meet for a beer and some good German food sometime again. He laughed a little and said he could not stay very long—he was going to dig for black opals. So I think I know where he would be going."

Illya nodded. "The opal fields a few hundred miles northwest of here."

"Not just the opal fields, my friend. The black opals are very rare and valuable. They come from only one area, and that is where I think he went. If he did not lie to me, you will find him there."

An U.N.C.L.E. six-place twinjet from the Sydney office with Illya at the wheel took them over the three hundred miles of mountains and desert in about forty-five minutes the next day, and set them down gently on a long patch of hard-baked earth. Lightning Ridge lies fifty miles beyond the railhead at Pokataroo, across the Barwon River. The town is a small collection of weather-beaten houses of paintless boards and hand-smeared adobe plaster, with a small dirt airstrip and a population of four or five hundred people. It is also the center of the only area in the world where true black opals are found.

The usually staid Encyclopedia Britannica describes this stone as combining "the iridescence of the dewdrop with the color of the rainbow, set in the blackness of night . . . a smothered mass of hidden fire." Looking at the one in Illya's hand, Napoleon could understand the writer's enthusiasm.

"It really is beautiful, isn't it?" said Suzie. "I wonder . . ."

"Sorry, ma'am," said the man behind the counter. "That's one I found myself, and it's part of what I expect to retire on someday."

Outside the little general store the yellow sand glowed hot in the desert noon, but inside the heavy windowless walls it was dark and reasonably comfortable. The three sat at a short rude counter with glasses of delicious Australian beer before them, talking casually with the manager, the owner, and the bartender.

Illya handed the opal back to him respectfully. "In the city, that would have to be kept under lock and key."

"Right. Then I wouldn't be able to look at it when I wanted to, and I'd 'ave to watch everybody else instead. One of the reasons I like it better out 'ere. Not many opals left now—they got pretty much mined out fifteen, twenty years ago. We find 'em lyin' about once in a while, though, and they still bring a good price in the Smoke."

"You get many tourists out here trying their luck?"

The Digger laughed. "Not likely. The last few days there 'ave been as many through as in the last six months. Countin' you, there must've been a couple dozen people. Some of 'em are 'ere still."

"Where?"

He pointed vaguely over his shoulder, indicating some place beyond the rough wood wall. "Roughing it. Two or three stayed when the rest left; they're camped down near the stream bed."

"Did one man come alone recently?" Illya asked. "A day or two ago?"

The Aussie looked at him thoughtfully. "Funny thing—t'other blokes asked that too."

"What did you tell them?"

"Not a thing, mate. In a town this size, people come and go and get lost in the crowds. We don't 'ave a registration center."

"Oh, stop it!" said Suzie, pulling out a photograph of Schneider. "We're looking for this man, and it's a matter of life and death that we find him before these other people do. They'll kill him!"

"Well, it might 'appen 'e'd know about it, wouldn't 'e? And likely would 'ave a few trustworthy people coverin' 'is trail for 'im. There's an awful lot of Outback for a man to get lost in—and stay lost if 'e don't want to be found."

"But we think he does," said Napoleon. "He left clues that would direct us here—left clues with his friends. It sounds as if these others are on his trail too, but they don't know where he is. We do. He came to Lightning Ridge yesterday or the day before. Whoever these others are—and we have a pretty good idea—they're obviously casting about all over the area looking for him."

"Well, Cobber . . . you might be too, y'know."

"But we aren't," said Suzie impatiently.

"Forget it," said Illya suddenly. "We're getting nowhere." Napoleon and Suzie looked at him as he said, "Diggers are stubborn—if they don't want to tell you something, you might as well talk to Ayres Rock." He finished his beer at a swallow, and started to the door. They followed him.

Once outside, he kept going. Napoleon caught up with him.

"You look as if you know what you're doing. Do you?"

"I think so. Kurt's friend in there mentioned some others who were here on the same mission—I thought we could get together with them and compare notes."

"You're kidding," said Suzie.

"I don't think he is," said Napoleon.

There were a few trees down along the dry watercourse a quarter of a mile or so west of town, and the three wandered along in their shade until a couple of olive-drab tents appeared before them.

"Not much of a field headquarters," said Napoleon.

"Convenient and practical," said Illya. "No rain this time of year, no large dangerous animals, not many bugs. Not Thrush, this time—they would not stoop to roughing it in this style."

"Now what do we do?" asked Suzie. "Walk up and knock on the tent flap?"

"Ordinarily, we should wait until night and drop in unexpectedly. But if they don't already know of our presence, they soon will and I'd just as soon get to them before they can radio for help. They're pretty serious about this search for Schneider, and there is probably a respectable force scattered over the surrounding hundred thousand square miles."

"My thought exactly," said Illya. "I don't think we should even bother to knock."

Traditional methods are usually the most effective. With guns drawn, the two U.N.C.L.E. agents stepped past the flap of the larger tent and addressed the backs of two men who crouched over a radio set in the corner. Both were dressed in khaki bush jackets and trousers, with high boots. Both were deeply engrossed in the operation of the bulky transmitter, and both turned suddenly at the voices behind them.

"Stand away from there," said Illya coldly. A glance at the meters on the case told him it was not yet in operation. "Keep your hands in sight."

With some hesitation they did as directed. "What is this?" said one of them truculently. "We have no money—no valuables for you to rob."

"Who were you calling?"

"We were not calling—we were listening for the weather report."

"On the 40-meter band? There are no official weather reports broadcast on that frequency—it's a moderate-range amateur band."

The face of the spokesman betrayed ingenuous surprise. "I must have had the adjustment wrong. No wonder we could not receive the storm warnings."

"You're not Australian," said Napoleon. "Who are you?"

"We are honest tourists from Egypt," said the spokesman. "His name is Abdul. My name is Rameses. He does not speak much English."

"Okay. Let us tell you a few things. You're here looking for a German sailor named Kurt Schneider. You're probably one part of a search covering a very wide area. You were just about to call someone on that radio. The only question I want an answer to is whether you were calling with a regular check-in, or to report your finding of the gentleman in question."

Rameses was well enough trained not to register surprise. Neither did he answer.

"Perhaps I can help, Napoleon," said Illya, glancing at his watch. "The time is exactly 1:36 P.M.—not a likely time for a regularly scheduled contact. Suzie—"

"Yes?"

"While Napoleon keeps these two company, you and I will check the other tent. I think you may find an old friend there."

Napoleon shifted his gun to cover both the Egyptians as his partner and the girl ducked out behind him. Their footsteps crunched softly away across the sun-baked dirt.

Rameses made another attempt. "Believe me, sir, we are only harmless tourists," he said, stepping slightly forward.

"That's fine," said Solo. "As long as you're harmless, so am I."

The one called Abdul also took a half step forward, at a divergent angle from his compatriot. Napoleon took a step back and felt the tent flap. "That's enough," he said sharply. "Sit down." This was the difficult point. He should probably have shot one in the leg—but they still just *might* really be innocent tourists. . . .

The two Egyptians exchanged a glance, and Rameses

made a sudden feinting move. Napoleon's gun hand swung automatically in his direction, and at that instant Abdul charged.

Solo sidestepped quickly, but a flailing arm caught him in the stomach and he doubled over. Rameses was on top of him at once, fumbling for his throat. He kept his chin tucked to his chest, and dropped to his knees, pulling the attacker over his head. Abdul had recovered from his bull-like charge and now leaped, just as Napoleon brought his U.N.C.L.E. Special up level and fired three times into the man's midsection. He made a few noises after he hit the ground, but kicked and then lay still after a few seconds. Rameses lay on his back where he had been thrown, and did not attempt to rise.

Then the tent flap was thrown aside and Illya's intense face thrust inside over the muzzle of his automatic. "What happened?"

"They stopped being harmless tourists," said Napoleon, his breath gradually returning. "One of them is now completely harmless, unless he harbored some loathsome disease."

Suzie appeared next to Illya. She looked down in horror. "Oh, Napoleon!" she said. "Did you have to kill him?"

"Possibly not. But the only way to have found out would have involved him killing me if I was wrong. And I consider myself more valuable than he was." He stood up and dusted his coat. "What did you find in the other tent?"

"A German sailor named Kurt Schneider, according to our identification expert here. He seems to be drugged. He's unconscious, at any rate, with no signs of injury."

Napoleon looked down at the surviving Egyptian, and nodded. "You have a lot of explaining to do," he said, and placed the still-warm muzzle of his automatic lightly against the back of the man's head. "We have all afternoon, and a boundless interest in hearing your life story in full detail. Now go ahead. Sing for us, Rameses—sing as if your life depended on it."

Chapter 8

"A Message From Space."

TWENTY-FIVE HOURS later it was almost midnight in Manhattan. A special jet had brought a party of five directly from Sydney, pausing to refuel in Hawaii and Los Angeles. They had slept during the trip, and now were alert and functioning again.

Napoleon and Illya shared their places around the conference table with Suzie, on whom the strain of the recent pace of events was beginning to tell. Alexander Waverly faced them across the round table, and had many things to say.

"Five days ago," he began, touching a button and illuminating a screen on the wall behind him, "a large satellite was observed by the Astronomical Tracking Station at Johannesburg. It appears to be the largest artificial object in orbit; I have been told by people whose business it is to know such things that it probably holds over one hundred men, and could easily carry a large number of nuclear or thermonuclear missiles."

A blurred, grainy photograph appeared on the screen —it showed a wheel-like shape with two opposed spokes and a tall hub against a background of stars. Waverly continued:

"It is approximately two hundred and fifty feet across. The tubular body of the satellite is therefore thirty or forty feet in diameter." He paused.

Napoleon looked puzzled. "I would have thought we would have heard about something that big. I take it that it isn't ours?"

"Not only that, Mr. Solo. Apparently it isn't anyone's. Neither the Russians nor the British nor the French have claimed it. The best guess so far is that it may be a Chinese effort, using Russian equipment, but they have made no statement to that effect so far, and this remains at best a doubtful hypothesis."

"It should have taken some time to build something that large," said Illya thoughtfully. "It would have to have been constructed in orbit—it simply is not structurally capable of standing the stresses of a rocket launching."

Napoleon cleared his throat tentatively. "Ah—has anyone thought that it might not have been launched from the Earth?"

Illya started to say, "Oh, *really,* Napoleon!" but he was cut off.

"Extraterrestrial origin?" Waverly nodded. "The idea has already been offered. It was under serious consideration, in fact, until the nature of the transmission from the Wheel changed, a day and a half ago."

"Changed? How?"

"Before it had merely been sending coded telemetric signals. Now . . ." Their superior touched another button, and a concealed speaker came to life. They heard the familiar twittering of telemetry, and then a voice began—definitely a human voice. It was male, baritone, and young.

"*Saluton, Tera Komandejo,*" it said. "*Jen Spaci-Stacio Unu, sendante sian unuan raporton reen al la Tero. La sipanaro alvenis sur la transport-sipoj sendifekte, kaj ciuj aparatoj ci tie funkcias bonege.*"

The voice continued in the same language. Suzie looked puzzled. "That sounds like Italian," she said, "but I don't understand it."

"It's Esperanto," said Illya. "An artificial language—the best-known of many. It's spoken and understood all over the world."

"What's he saying?"

"He started by identifying himself as 'Space-Station One,' and this as the first report to Earth, saying the crew had arrived on the shuttle ships safely, and all systems there were functioning perfectly. Now he's talking about the view. He says they're crossing the dawn line over Nepal, and only the peaks of the Himalayas are touched with the sunlight, so they stand out like signal fires against the darkness that still lies in the valleys . . ."

Waverly touched another button and the voice stopped. "The Wheel has maintained voice transmission approximately two-thirds of the time since. It has all been recorded, and has been subjected to intensive analysis by Section Four. There has been no indication in any of the material of any specific national origin."

He leaned back and fumbled for his pipe. Napoleon, Illya and Suzie sat erect, staring at the projection of the Monster Wheel. Finally Napoleon spoke:

"Do you think the mysterious rocket launching site we're after could be involved in this problem too?"

"There's an ancient saying in my country," said Illya, "to the effect that when you have two pieces of a jigsaw puzzle that will fit nowhere else, they may fit together."

"Ancient saying?"

"Comparatively ancient."

Waverly returned to the conversation, having completed his own project, which was now smoldering between his teeth. He took it out, and replaced it with a statement:

"That monstrous wheel represents possibly the greatest threat to the security of the entire world in history. Whoever controls it can control any spot on the surface of the planet except for a few thousand square miles at the poles. From such a stable platform, every major operation can be studied with relatively simple telescopes, and thermonuclear missiles can be placed with a maximum of accuracy and a minimal expenditure of energy. And as long as we don't know who controls *it*, we remain unable to strike back."

"Couldn't we send a missile up to the Wheel?" asked Suzie.

"They could track it and destroy it at their leisure—and destroy as well its launching site and the nation that launched it."

The two agents considered this for a while. Illya finally spoke: "That seems to leave us with only one choice."

Napoleon nodded. "Find *their* launching site."

"Exactly," said Waverly. He glanced at Suzie. "And I'm afraid I must insist you do it alone. I understand your personal involvement in this operation, Miss Danz, but this is a job for professional personnel." He turned back to the two men.

"Section Three has filed an interrogation report on your Egyptian trophy. He stood up quite well as far as we dared go with him—gave only his name and nationality, and insisted that his rights under international law were being violated. He was right, of course—they were. We confronted him with the photos we have of the Monster Wheel, though, and they seemed to catch him off balance."

Waverly paused to inspect his pipe, which seemed to have gone out. He took his time puffing its dormant embers back into life, and then spoke again. "He claimed it belonged to his own nation."

"To Egypt!" said three voices simultaneously.

"To Egypt. The interrogators pointed out to him that this was obviously ridiculous, but he continued to insist for a few exchanges, then suddenly shut up. He said if his government hadn't seen fit to announce it to the world, he would respect their judgment. And they could get nothing more out of him.

"Also, Mr. Schneider has recovered rather well from the drugs he was given in Australia. And we are now in possession on the coördinates of the mysterious island."

"Have we identified it?" asked Illya.

"Yes, we have. Few charts bother to list it, since it is tiny, uninhabited, has no natural fresh water, and is far off the main trade routes. It is a volcanic island, with a single peak at two thousand and some feet above sea level. The last reported activity of the volcano was in 1872. It is now officially considered extinct. The island itself is moderately jungled, and is roughly two miles from east to west, three miles north to south.

"A photo-reconnaissance aircraft has been ordered over the island—more than one would probably arouse the suspicions of anyone who might be there and equipped to observe it. The results of the mission will be in our hands by tomorrow afternoon, and a topographical map will be prepared for your use.

"Friday you will depart by jet to our branch office in Colombo, Ceylon, where you will board a special ship. You will be put over the side in a miniature submarine some two hundred miles from the island, and will proceed to infiltrate whatever operation may be centered there. Obtain as much information as you can regarding the nature and especially the source of supply for the operation, and get out again. You will then be picked up by the same ship at the spot you left it. All details beyond these will be left to your own discretions."

"Fine," said Napoleon crisply. "We'll want camouflage suits, some basic guerrilla equipment and survival gear. Also two scuba outfits. And if at all possible, a map of underwater contours around the island. We'll want to sink the sub in fifty or a hundred feet of water, where it'll be safe while we're ashore."

"Section Five will get to work on the map tonight. Incidentally, you should plan to spend tomorrow down in the Research Department. Mr. Simpson will want to check you out on the new submarine."

"That shouldn't be necessary, sir, unless it's a radical departure from the old one."

"It is. Top submerged speed of forty knots plus, depth capability in excess of five thousand feet, and totally noiseless."

"Five thousand feet? Why weren't we using that on the H-bomb that got lost off Spain last spring?"

"Too much publicity attendant, and the fact that it was still in the final stages of construction at the time. It has now been extensively tested, although this will be its first real use in the field."

"A top speed of forty knots, and completely noiseless?" asked Illya. "How is that accomplished?"

Waverly held up a patient hand. "These technical matters are outside my bailiwick," he said, "and it is past midnight. I suggest you take up your questions with Mr. Simpson tomorrow."

"Just one more question. . . ."

"Yes?"

"The name of the island."

"Oh, of course. The only two charts it appears on call it Dauringa Island. No reason for the name—probably some obscure navigator who first sighted it."

"Dauringa Island," mused Napoleon. "A peaceful enough name. Palm trees waving in a gentle tropical breeze. But somehow I have the feeling it will not live up to the travel posters."

Illya nodded. "It may even look peaceful on the surface, Napoleon—but not deep down inside, where it really counts."

Section III : "Round And Round Went The Monster Wheel . . ."

Chapter 9

"This Is *Your* Submarine—Keep It Clean."

THE RESEARCH AND DEVELOPMENT section of U.N.C.L.E. in New York is in the very lowest level of the building, which extends nearly as far down into the solid bedrock of Manhattan Island as it does up into the polluted air. This level includes the target range, the main emergency generator plant, and the docks which open onto the river.

In the great echoing vault of the construction area, the lights hung far overhead and shed their cold light over half an acre of heavy machinery, machinists, and their products.

One product rested, fat and shining, in a cradle on the floor at one side of the room. It was a dull gray teardrop about fifteen feet through at its widest and some thirty feet long. At the center of the rounded end was a small porthole, with a ring of lights around it. All the surfaces were flush with the metal, leaving the curve unbroken. Here and there on the hull were small areas of different textures which could be recognized as transducers, presumably for sonar or similar detection systems, as well as a number of screened openings and small access hatches. Just above the porthole was a large screened opening—an intake scoop of some kind.

About halfway from the fattest part to the rounded nose a ring of small openings girdled the entire object. And partway back towards the tapering tail, on the top, a three-foot circle showed where an access hatch was located. A ladder led up the side of the cradle to the hatch, which was closed.

Napoleon Solo stood at the nose of the thing, hands cupped around his face, peering through the porthole into the darkened interior. Illya stood behind him, with a thin dark man in a white lab smock, who was speaking.

"Some years ago, experiments were being made by medical researchers in the design of blood-pumps for a new design of artificial heart. They were interested in a pump that would not break down under years of constant use. In the course of their tests they discovered that a powerful enough electromagnetic field could affect the blood directly, and move it through tubes without the use of motors or impellers of any kind. Since sea water is electrically quite similar to blood, it was reasoned that the same electromagnetic flux could be used to move it. Stewart Way, of Westinghouse, developed the basic principle just this summer at Santa Barbara."

Napoleon took his face away from the porthole and wiped the fog of his breath off it with his sleeve. "So that's why the submarine is noiseless. No motor—no moving parts—just an electrical field to pump sea water. That means it's jet-propelled."

"Like a squid," said Illya. "It takes in sea water and squirts it out again."

"Exactly," said the inventor. "That is the reason for naming it the Squid. It is a prototype of what will someday be called the Squid class of submarines." He cleared his throat and smiled shyly. "More modest than calling it the Simpson class."

"Does it squirt ink too?" asked Napoleon.

"We thought that would be unnecessary. Most undersea combat is carried out by sound rather than by sight."

"Have you worked out a way of making it invisible to sonar, then?" asked Illya.

Simpson nodded. "More or less. The propulsion system itself does a great deal to help that."

Napoleon had wandered around to the pointed end

of the submarine, and was looking around, slightly puzzled. "Where's the jet?" he asked. "This end looks solid to me."

"It is. The jets are up here," said the man in the lab coat, pointing to the ring around the nose of the teardrop.

Illya looked at them closely. "I thought those were maneuvering jets. They seem to point straight out to the sides."

"They do," said Simpson. "The electromagnetic impeller drives the water out through this ring at right angles to the direction of travel."

Napoleon wandered back in time to hear this, and held up his hand for a moment. "Right angles, huh? Then what makes the thing go forward?"

"It's called the Coanda effect. Don't ask me why it works—I'm an engineer, not a scientist."

"But you built it; you should understand it."

"I didn't exactly build it myself—an analogue computer designed the hull from the Coanda equations, the outer hull was built by the construction unit here, the inner pressure hull was built in France, the control systems were prepared by our electronics department, the power system came from General Atomics, and a specialist work crew put them all together here."

Napoleon pondered this for a moment, then finally asked, "But what do *you* have to do with the submarine, then?"

Simpson smiled and shrugged a little. "Well . . . I'm not sure. All I know is that they didn't build things like this before I came here."

"Oh," said Napoleon, nodding firmly as though he now understood the whole operation.

"Anyway," Simpson continued, "basically, the vortex flow created by the jet of water—or air; the design works on airplanes, too—follows the curve of the side. It goes around the bulge, and trails off towards the tail. The flow all comes together at the tip, and pushes the whole thing in the opposite direction. As it starts to move, the flow bends more backward, and the water that flows past is pulled in with the jets, adding to the volume of the flow."

Illya shook his head. "It seems that would waste a lot of the energy in turbulence. Wouldn't it be simpler and more efficient just to direct the flow out the rear in the traditional manner?"

"Simplicity is not always the same as efficiency. This particular design is roughly 65% more efficient than the same amount of energy directed out the stern. Dr. Coanda's equations indicate a theoretical limit of approximately twice the efficiency, but we don't have the design capability yet.

"Incidentally, because of the nature of the flow, there is very little turbulence. Instead of wasting energy in cavitation, as most submarines do, the flow is directed around the vehicle and used for additional propulsive energy. The mass of water that you would ordinarily have to butt your way through is pulled aside by the Coanda jets.

"This gives you a shell of moving water, inside which your submarine floats. And because of the pressure differential in the flow, as long as you are moving, sonar will be refracted around you rather than bouncing off. You will, in effect, be invisible. Of course, when you slow down or stop, the pressures will equalize and you will reappear. Any more questions?"

The two U.N.C.L.E. agents looked up at the Coanda Squid. It rested in its cradle like a finless bomb, with the distant blue-white tubes of the overhead fluorescents casting distorted highlights on its bulging surface. Solo remembered something his partner had once said: "Personally, I believe color television to be impossible too. But since it does exist, I will act as if I believed in it."

He said so. Illya glanced at him, and smiled wryly. The last time he had said that they had been faced with another device, for which no published equations existed, and which was to be used against them—and the rest of the world—by their enemies. This submarine, on the other hand, did have sound, recognized scientific principles behind it. But then, so did color television.

"Napoleon," he said, "you have simply got to learn to move with the times. So many marvels are constantly being invented, you should learn to accept them."

"Illya, you know I just have a naturally inquisitive mind. Besides, I like to know how things work before I trust my life to them."

Illya nodded. "Let's take a look inside."

They ducked under the cradle, and opened the lower hatch. As they did so, Simpson pointed out the door hinge. "The bearing here is lubricated by the sea water itself," he said. "It reacts with the material to form a smooth film. The greater the pressure, the more efficient the lubrication. One at a time in the airlock, please. You may find it a little crowded with three in the pressure hull, but there will be enough room to see."

Napoleon followed him, and found a metal tube which appeared to run the whole height of the submarine, to the matching hatch on the top. There were hand grips along the sides, and partway up he found another hatch open on the forward side of the tube. He pulled himself up and through this, and found himself in one side of a sphere. The walls were lined with gear, with three bunks folded up against one side. A small partition shielded a chemical toilet, and next to the bunks a tiny sink and an electric stove made a compact but efficient galley.

Two control seats, contoured and equipped with safety harnesses, bracketed the inner orifice of the porthole. Both panel layouts seemed identical, with sonar display screens, and matching controls. The sub was apparently maneuvered like an airplane—the wheels and pedals looked the same, and Napoleon recognized rate-of-climb, turn-and-bank, and similar aerial indicators.

Illya joined them, and after a quick look over the living facilities went straight to the control board. He fitted himself into the righthand seat and tried out the wheel, reached experimentally for the controls, and nodded satisfaction when he found them all comfortably within an arm radius.

Napoleon climbed up to the other seat, and found it a good fit. Simpson stood between them. "Is everything satisfactory?" he asked.

"So far," said Illya. "What's our cruising range, and how long is the oxygen supply?"

"Range of this model is only about a thousand miles. The tanks carry air for nine days for two people, six days for three. This is considering eight hours of sleeping per day, no smoking, and no prolonged violent exertion. You will, of course, be completely checked out on the control systems. Any questions before we start?"

"Yes," said Illya. "The bearings in the doors are lubricated only by sea water; the electromagnetic pumping system will work only on sea water. In other words, this would be useless in fresh water."

Simpson thought quite a while. "Well . . ." he said at last, "you're right. It will work perfectly only in one particular environment, even though it *is* a large environment. But in case of emergency, this gauge here"—he pointed—"reads the salinity of the water. Should it drop towards the red zone, you are coming into an area of fresh water, such as might be caused by the outflow of the mouth of a large river, or an undersea spring. It also trips a buzzer, which can be turned off by this button below the gauge, as warning. Until we develop some more radical departures, you will have to be content with this.

"Incidentally, should it become necessary, you do have small auxiliary motors to pump the water out the propulsion vents in a more conventional manner, but I'm afraid they do make a small amount of noise. Yes, Mr. Solo?"

"Ah—I notice the speed indicator has three sets of calibrations on it: knots, kilometers per hour, and miles per day. Why?"

"Well, I put knots there because this is, after all, a ship of sorts. Kilometers per hour is the international standard measure of speed. And I added miles per hour because that's what I think in. Also, this way you won't have to do conversions in your head."

"What about me?" said Illya. "I'm Russian. For me you should have a speed meter calibrated in versts per hour."

Simpson shrugged. "It's only three cents more for an extra meter face, after all."

Illya grinned at Napoleon, who shared his little joke, and appreciated the technician's comeback. Without further comment, they went on to discuss the inertial guidance system, which handled most of the navigation for the Squid.

Their checkout occupied the rest of the day, including a break for lunch, which was prepared from the freeze-dried concentrates in the Squid's stores and cooked up on the electric stove. By the time the clock on the instrument panel read 2200 GMT, which Napoleon's electric wrist watch translated as 5:00 P.M. they had learned a good deal about the internal functioning of the sub.

The following day they took it out into the East River (which is actually a salt-water tidal estuary rather than a true fresh-water river, which would have interfered with the operation of the Squid) and with Simpson guiding them they cruised submerged through the murky waters of the Upper Bay, and then east past Coney Island and Rockaway Point. Both Napoleon and Illya spent a pleasurable afternoon handling the sub, and leaving and entering the airlock in scuba gear while submerged.

When they returned, wet and exhausted, to the secret

harbor under U.N.C.L.E. Headquarters that evening, a message from Waverly awaited them.

After briefly refreshing themselves, they reported to the familiar office on the topmost level. Their superior looked up from his work to greet them and inquire about their progress. The necessary amenities disposed of, he continued, "Something new has come up on your current assignment. I have the tape somewhere around here of the latest broadcast from the Monster Wheel—but if you don't understand Esperanto I can tell you roughly what it said.

"First let me explain that there has recently been some discussion—on a very high level, of course, and terribly secret—of attempting to fire a missile at the Wheel. Sometime this morning, apparently, the Wheel began voice transmission again. Without addressing anyone in particular, it stated in so many words that any missile approaching within twenty kilometers would be considered hostile, and the nation that had launched it would be bombarded with thermonuclear devices from space."

He paused while his two top agents looked at each other, and raised two pairs of eyebrows slightly. Then he continued, a slight tone of annoyance creeping into his voice. "They concluded by saying that they had made no threats to any nation, and had broken no laws, but they would defend themselves if attacked. And of course as far as that goes they're correct. There's no law in the world against launching a space station without a license. Nor is there any that says you must identify your space stations. But every one of the governments represented by the United Network Command is biting its collective fingernails and urging me to do something about this menace in the sky."

He snorted and leaned back in his chair. "You understand my position. All I can do is make the situation clear to you, and urge your greatest efficiency and most careful work. And this is unnecessary, because you work at peak efficiency most of the time anyway. If you didn't, you wouldn't be in the positions you now occupy."

"Exactly," said Napoleon. "We'd be sitting behind a nice safe desk somewhere."

Waverly's face wrinkled into a wry smile. "There are times, Mr. Solo, when I would gladly trade this nice safe desk of mine for a good simple field assignment. Out there, at least, you are allowed to shoot back when you are attacked. Here there is no protection, and no retaliation." He shook his head. "But to return to the subject. I would like to accelerate the operation by a day, if possible. How would you feel about taking off for Ceylon tomorrow, instead of Friday? It will give you a day less to practice with the submarine, but Simpson's reports on your work have been most complimentary. How do you feel?"

They nodded simultaneously, and Napoleon spoke. "If you have the aerial survey maps, and the underwater contour maps we'll need, we can take off any time."

"They are ready, and will be here in my office for you tomorrow morning. You can spend the day making your final preparations. The jet leaves Kennedy International at four P.M. It's not a regular commercial flight, but a cargo plane. The submarine will accompany you disguised as several automobiles."

"I suppose it's too late to make one change in the submarine," said Illya slowly. "Not a major one—more a design revision than anything else."

They looked at him questioningly.

"Gray is such a drab color. How much more appropriate if it could be painted yellow."

"Appropriate? And why yellow?"

"Oh, never mind," said Illya. "It was just an idea. . . ."

Chapter 10

"Island Ho!"

AFTER LUNCH the Captain conducted Napoleon Solo and Illya Kuryakin below decks and unlocked the doors in the "D" hold. The harsh incandescents overhead cast black shadows and sharp highlights around the small chamber, and left a pool of inky blackness under the Squid, which hung in a double canvas sling a few feet above the floor.

The ship in which they had left Colombo some three days ago was a disreputable-looking freighter, flying the Liberian flag, but owned and operated, sometimes at a profit, by the United Network Command for Law and Enforcement. It usually worked as a real freighter, but was maintained as a cover for a number of unusual operations, for which it was specially outfitted. "D" hold was only one of the many special features of the ship. Only her captain was privy to all the surprises contained by her hull, and his U.N.C.L.E. rank was not much lower than Solo's own.

Down in the damp darkness of the hold, the mini-sub swung gently in her canvas cradle, awaiting the kiss of the salt water that would bring her to life. Inside her dull gray body rested maps, supplies and equipment that would direct and sustain two valuable men for an indefinite period of time—underwater, and ashore in a hostile land.

The ship's engines were idling now, and the time had come for parting. Napoleon and Illya slipped through the hatch in the underside of the Squid, with a last look around at the dim interior of the hold—the smell of rust, the patches of moss on the walls, and the bearded captain standing near the door, awaiting their signal.

And then they were inside. The slight pressure change

on his eardrums told Napoleon that the outer hatch had been sealed, and a moment later Illya's blond head appeared in the airlock.

"Welcome aboard, Captain Kuryakin," he said formally.

"Thank you, Captain Solo," said the Russian agent, as he slipped into his padded control seat and fastened the safety straps.

At the same time, Napoleon lifted a small microphone from a clip below the board, thumbed the button on the side, and said, "Hello, Mother Ship. Squid is ready to go."

A speaker next to the mike-slip hissed to life. "Hello, Squid. Your signal clear. All set." The lights outside the little sub blinked out, and a moment later, as Illya touched a button, their own headlights blazed to life. " 'D' hold sealed," said the speaker. "Open 'er up."

Faintly through the double hull of the submarine Napoleon could hear a low rumble of heavy machinery. Leaning forward, his head next to Illya's, he peered out through their little porthole into the vast hollow of the hold.

The floor was bubbling up, blue and sparkling, beneath them. The deck plates were drawing back into the bulkheads, and the sea, carrying the hot equatorial afternoon sunlight around the bulk of the ship, surged up under their plastic craft. It stopped a few feet below the porthole, and the speaker hissed again.

"Pressure in 'D' hold equalized. Bleed air."

Smoothly now the level began to rise. Illya turned off their headlights again as a bright line of surface crawled upwards across the window, and the Squid began to quiver as the water took her weight. She rocked slightly as she floated free of the cradle sling, and meters sprang to life as Napoleon closed the switches that began the powerful electromotive forces driving sea water out through the Coanda ring. The two agents felt a gentle surge as the Squid slipped out of her sling, and

Napoleon slid a lever slowly forward. Tanks of ballast began to flood, and the walls of the hold seemed to move upward around them. Then the hull of the ship was suddenly floating above them, and the blue-green light flooded into their pressure sphere. Napoleon thumbed the microphone button again.

"Squid away," he said. "We'll see you right here in a few days."

"A-Okay, Squid," said the metallic voice under the control panel. "Stay out of trouble, and write if you get work."

"So long, Mother Ship."

"Back to radio silence, now," said Illya to Napoleon, a tone of caution in his voice.

"Squid out," said Napoleon, and replaced the microphone.

On two of his display screens, a long oval blob indicated the freighter, already two hundred yards behind them and a hundred feet above. The Squid continued to sink, aiming for a cruising depth of a thousand feet. Soon the inside lights were switched on, as the illumination from outside dropped through the spectrum past blue and green and finally out of the visual range altogether.

They leveled off some two-tenths of a mile below the sparkling waves, secure in the knowledge of more than two miles between them and the bottom, and Illya set the course at 195°. An automatic sonar watch would alert them if anything as large as themselves showed on their screens, or if an uncharted sea-mount should loom nearby. Napoleon leaned back for a nap. The chairs were comfortable, and they would probably have no place to sleep tonight.

"You ought to get some sleep too," he told Illya. "We have five hours to go before we come up on that island, and it's going to be a busy night."

"In a few minutes. You go ahead and I'll join you. I want to check our drift rate. The South Equatorial Current goes west at a knot and a half around here, and I don't want to miss our island by nine miles."

Napoleon woke up some time later to the smell of food. He looked first at his board, and saw they were still under way, at reduced speed, but the bottom was rising gradually. There was something showing on the edge of his scope, and he extended the range to its limits, regardless of lost definition.

Some ten miles ahead of them the bottom rose past their present depth and broke the surface over a space of two or three miles. He leaned back in his contour seat and declaimed in a properly nautical tone, "Island ho! Dead ahead at ten miles."

"You just noticed it?" asked Illya dryly. "We'll be grounding at the hundred-foot level in another twenty minutes. I thought we should have a bite of hot nourishing supper before we go ashore. Accommodations there are likely to be limited."

"A good thought. What have you whipped up in your modern all-electronic miracle kitchen?"

"I don't know. There's no name on the package—just a description of the contents in unappetizing technical terms. But it's well-balanced for a maximum of nutrition and a minimum of bulk, and it smells edible."

"That's all I ask. This salt air always gives me an appetite." Napoleon slipped out of his chair and accepted the tray Illya handed him.

They ate and drank, and filled their canteens from the fresh water supply. Then the depth alarm began to sound softly, and they returned to the control panels. In a few minutes a rocky bottom jagged with coral showed in their headlights, and the Squid settled gently to rest. A panel of switches were clicked over, and meters fell back against their stop pins as the electromagnetic fields collapsed and died.

A few fish swam idly past, attracted by the light. One or two paused to stare through the porthole at the strange exhibit within, then passed on like idle tourists at an aquarium.

Finally all was ready. The outside lights were doused; the cabin lights were set so a radio signal from above could turn them on to light the returning travelers home. Both agents slipped their packs on over their wet-suits. Napoleon crawled into the airlock and sealed the inner hatch behind him. In the yellow illumination of his underwater torch he adjusted his face-mask, and touched the button beside the hatch. With scarcely a sound, a cool pressure began rising about him. The black surface crept up and surrounded him as he hung in the three-foot cylindrical airlock.

When the lock was full, he swallowed several times as the weight of a hundred feet of sea water squeezed his eardrums and his chest. The pressure was high, but if they got to the surface with reasonable despatch there would be insufficient time for nitrogen to dissolve in their bloodstreams necessitating gradual and tedious decompression. The inside of the sub was kept close to surface normal pressure for just this reason.

He let himself float to the top hatch, worked the dogs, and pushed it open. Then he was out, looking down at the dimly visible shape of the submarine. He waggled his fins, and swam around to the front.

Peering back in through the port, he could see Illya standing, masked and finned, next to the lock entrance, watching the indicator lights. The bottom one flashed green, and he followed Solo. Napoleon swam back to meet him.

It was almost a minute before the hatch opened and the Russian pulled himself out. His light swung around and joined his partner's, and side by side they swam along the bottom as it slanted upwards.

It was shortly after dusk when they broke the surface. The sub had been grounded at the opposite end of the island from the volcanic cone, and the U.N.C.L.E.

agents surfaced quietly a hundred yards off-shore for cautious reconnaissance.

Their eyes, accustomed to the underwater darkness, could see the shore easily by the last of the sky glow. It looked deserted.

Treading water, they conferred in whispers. "No reason to think we might have been spotted. I'll go in first —signal you if it's all clear."

Illya nodded and submerged again. Napoleon replaced his scuba mouthpiece and began stroking steadily along, a few feet below the surface.

In a matter of minutes, he felt the tug of surf about him and rose again. The half-moon overhead showed him lines and curves of white froth against black sand. The surf was low, and except for the passage of the foam, his black wet-suit would be nearly invisible against the beach. He ducked under a wave and started his landing.

Water surged about him and spun him once while he fought to recover his balance, and then the sand scraped against his knees. He grabbed for it and pushed himself erect, then stumbled up the slope towards the trees some ten or fifteen feet before dropping flat.

He spat out the breathing valve and took his first lungful of natural air in several hours. Next he slipped the mask off his face and rubbed at his eyes. They itched from the pressure and a little sea water that had got in through the not-quite-perfect seal around his face. And he listened.

He listened while he continued removing his gear, and heard nothing. A few insects chittered, and a nightbird screeched, but the noises were natural and reassuring—the presence of alien intruders in the area would have damped the sounds.

After three minutes he pointed his flash out to sea and waved it in a circle. There was no answer. A minute later he repeated the signal. This time a spot of light flicked twice.

Two minutes later Illya was standing beside him in

the shelter of the trees. In silence they shucked out of their wet-suits, slipped on the camouflage coveralls from their packs, and blacked their faces. A few more minutes' work concealed their scuba gear under a foot of soft earth at the base of a distinguishable tree, and they were ready to complete their invasion.

Three cautious hours later they lay on their bellies in the brush and looked up at the side of the volcano. It rose up from beds of old lava, where a few hardy bushes had already managed to take root, and stood black and jagged against the moon-blue sky.

They had seen no signs of human habitation—if this island had been the launching site of a space missile, it was kept quite secure. No tracks, no cigarette butts, not even a smell of anything but the highly pungent Kerguelen's Land cabbage which grew in profusion among the scattered trees.

"There we are," said Napoleon in a whisper. "And it looks as if nobody's home."

"It seems a shame to come all this way and then leave without seeing them," said his partner. "Let's look for a door."

"They may be trying to avoid us—what if they don't answer the bell?"

"We sneak around and go in the window?"

Napoleon nodded, and they began moving off around the mountain, scanning the rock walls for openings of any kind.

Eventually it was a spark of light against the shadowed rocks that showed the door they were after. Illya spotted it first, tapped Napoleon, and pointed silently. Solo nodded, and they turned up the slope towards it, rubber-soled shoes soundless on the lava sheet as they climbed.

Then they saw another light—a match that flared in the darkness ahead of them. They froze in their tracks and sank flat against the harsh surface of the bare rock.

The match illuminated a man's face as it touched the end of his cigarette, and dimmed as he drew the flame into the tobacco. A moment later a voice was heard, softly, in English:

"God, but it's good to get out in the fresh air once in a while. I feel like a ruddy prisoner in there."

The match was blown out and the second smoker muttered agreement. "Sometimes I think they're a little crackers on security. There's nobody in a thousand miles that's not been checked and cross-checked by Thrush six ways from Sunday. But we're supposed to act like we're under siege every minute. Practically have to twist arms to get a blinkin' surface pass." He snorted. "In six months, what have we ever seen on radar? Three planes and one ship. And we sank the ship."

The two smoked in silence for a time, while the two U.N.C.L.E. agents huddled in their own shadows not fifty feet from them. Only a small portion of Napoleon's mind appreciated the irony—most of his attention was occupied in an attempt to make himself invisible.

After several minutes one of the glowing butts arched away into the darkness and burst in a shower of dying sparks. It was followed by a muttered curse. "Forgot again!" said the voice, and he started down the hill towards where the cigarette had fallen.

Napoleon and Illya lay very still and watched the silhouette of the Thrush moving diagonally, somewhat closer to them. But his attention was focused only on his error. Apparently nothing was allowed to be thrown where it could be seen from outside.

He struck another match and searched for the dead butt. When it burned down to his fingers he swore, dropped it, swore again, lit another, and picked up the first one. Then he found the butt and hurried back up the hill to his companion. "Got it," he said. "I don't know whether I'll be able to get the hang of this security nonsense or not. Force of habit keeps taking over."

The other one laughed shortly, stubbed his cigarette

out on the rock wall, and said, "Well, we've had our freedom for tonight. Let's get back inside."

The two men faded back into blackness under an overhang of rock, and were gone.

After a few moments, two blobs of shadow rose cautiously from the ground and crept up to the overhang. Even close up the U.N.C.L.E. agents could distinguish no back to the cave it formed. They stepped in.

There was a feeling of space ahead of them, and a breath of warm air smelling of oil and people moved gently past them. They nodded to each other in the darkness, and slowly and silently began to move down the long tunnel into the heart of the mountain.

Chapter 11

"Get Those Intruders!"

EVENTUALLY THE LAST of the tropical moonlight faded behind them, and Illya brought out his pocket flashlight. Putting his mouth to Napoleon's ear, he said softly, "I'm going to try the light for a second. Get ready to run."

He aimed the slender cylinder at the floor and pressed the button, tensed and alert for the sound of a guard who would probably shoot at the light. A few seconds passed, and nothing happened. He swung the dim beam up and along the wall, dilated pupils straining to draw in the faint images.

The walls were natural stone, only slightly smoothed in the excavating that had formed the tunnel. Not a door nor a side passage nor a ventilator broke the rough stone as far as he could see. After a few seconds they both moved forward again.

The diffused glow of the pocket light slipped along the lava floor and danced up the walls as they continued their stygian way for what seemed like several minutes. Then an answering glow became visible ahead, and they stopped.

"Well," murmured Napoleon, "I think we've arrived."

"Do we burst in without knocking?"

"I think not. Scarcely polite, not to say probably suicidal. Let's practice our sneaking technique."

"Fine. Keep that quiet pistol of yours handy; we may need to hush someone quickly, and I still haven't seen you use it."

"You've got a silencer—you can be just as quiet as I can."

"Yes, but you went to so much trouble bringing that rocket pistol it would be a shame not to let you use it."

"All right. If we have a choice, I'll go ahead. But if we don't, please don't stand on ceremony."

"Do I ever?"

Napoleon had to admit it was not one of Illya's characteristics, and they moved on.

Used air was still blowing softly in their faces, and they were hoping for a ventilator shaft to give them access to the interior of this sub-volcanic antheap. But it was beginning to appear that ventilation passed in and out through the same passages as personnel in search of a breath of fresh air and a cigarette. This meant a likelihood of guards and similar unpleasant phenomena in the immediate offing.

They stopped.

Napoleon shook his head thoughtfully. "It doesn't seem reasonable," he said, "to have all the foul air in the place blowing out from an inhabited area. Either there are blower vents between us and the lighted area, or the lights are leaking in from adjoining rooms where inhabitation is going on. I think it's worth looking at, anyway."

"Why not?" said Illya. "It's your idea—you go first."

"You've got the light."

"You don't need it now."

Napoleon proceeded, hand on his pistol.

The light did indeed grow stronger—the blue-green of fluorescent tubes somewhere. Then there was a corner in front of them. Both stopped, and Napoleon, who was still in the lead, extended an eye around the end of the wall.

There was a double-width steel door some ten feet farther down to the right of their passage, with eye-level glass panels in each half. Only light could be seen through them. The passage ended there.

He drew back and motioned Illya forward. "We're here," he said. "Take a look."

His partner did, and nodded, then moved cautiously around the corner. A moment later the two agents were looking through the glass panels of the doors into a steel-walled corridor, painted a soft green, lined with single doors, and apparently deserted. The corridor ended at a crossing passage about a hundred feet away.

Very gently, Illya tried the door. It remained closed. Napoleon raised one fist and pantomimed knocking. Illya shook his head, and began looking around the walls. Napoleon knew what he was thinking—that stale air had been blowing from somewhere.

They found the opening almost immediately—no great feat, since it was three feet square and set in the ceiling a few feet above their heads just at the corner of the tunnel.

It was the work of a few moments to undo the bolts at the four corners and lower the grille gently to the floor. Then Napoleon boosted Illya up into the hole overhead, tied a length of nylon rope from his pack around a corner of the grille and handed it up to his partner, who tucked the end in his teeth, leaving both hands free to pull him up into the air duct.

Together they hauled the grille back up from the floor, and used short lengths of rope to fasten it in place. A cursory examination from below would spot the change, but few people normally look over their heads, especially when bad air is blowing down upon them. Adding to this the dialogue they had heard outside, indicating that use of this passage was fairly uncommon, they felt reasonably secure in their jury-rigged arrangement.

Air-conditioning ducts are one of the most popular literary devices to enable the passage of persons, things and sounds from one point to another within a building, and as such have practically replaced the secret passages popular with another generation of novelists. But in actual practice, their very popularity has tended to defeat them. Most modern buildings include in their ventilating designs long verticals, baffles, internal grilles and occasional driving fans, all of which present moderate to severe problems for the casual tourist.

It was therefore a stroke of fortune that this particular installation had none of these internal protective devices. Napoleon didn't think to comment on it, feeling that his partner would share his conclusion that under the circumstances it was probably the Thrush builders had gone for efficiency rather than absolute safety. The island itself was certainly well enough protected, and the intake of the system was probably hidden quite well high above them on the mountainside. So there should have been no need for the usual security measures. And this was only reasonable—they couldn't have forseen the positive brilliance of the U.N.C.L.E. technical staff and agents that had not only found the secret island base, but managed to evade all the other protective devices and carry the conflict home to the enemy.

Napoleon Solo was feeling perhaps a little too confident as he crept along the metal tunnel. There was a constant humming, a deep-pitched vibration that came to them through the steel walls and shook the air around them so gently it had to be listened for consciously. Somewhere machinery was working—probably an electrical generating plant.

Small grilles opened occasionally beside them, and smaller side passages branched off. But there was no secondary tunnel, and they stayed with the main route. Each grille had to be checked carefully—if anyone happened to be looking at it as they went by, he might justifiably become curious.

The first two dozen rooms they looked into were empty. They appeared to be private quarters—small rooms, with a desk, a bed and a washstand, like a college dorm or the cheaper rooms at a YMCA. A small loudspeaker on the wall above the bed was the only standard decoration, but some of the rooms exhibited prints of widely varied types. Some sported pin-ups of assorted nationalities, some favored abstracts, and some preferred subject matter of a more technical nature. Three walls carried large representations of a von Braun-type space station, reënforcing the theory that the Monster Wheel had indeed been launched from this site. But only residential areas passed the view of the two U.N.C.L.E. agents.

Finally the duct branched and they stopped. "Now where?" asked Illya. Their choices angled vertically—one up and one down.

"Down, I think," said Napoleon. "The laboratories will probably be the deepest level, for security reasons, as well as protection of delicate gear against blast-off vibration and possible explosions."

"A properly-regulated launching site wouldn't have any explosions," said the Russian, as they started down the tube on hands and knees.

It was a long time before a duct opened into a room on either side of them. But when at last a square of light showed in the darkness, it proved to have been worth waiting for. Below them were rows of drafting tables, with work still in progress taped neatly to the slanting boards and T-squares hanging ready at their sides for the next day's work. Only a few lights were on here—presumably a skeleton staff might appear, or occasional guards wandered through.

Illya, straining his vision through the wire mesh, could

make out electronic circuitry on some of the drawing boards and construction designs on some others. He set about removing the screen.

At length both of them dropped lightly to the poured concrete floor, landing with flexed knees and falling into crouches behind the nearest tables. They waited thus for a minute or more, expecting the sounds of alarm to warn them of some detection system tripped or guard alerted by their presence. But silence remained about them.

As they waited, Illya's trained eyes scanned the walls and ceiling in his range of vision for concealed television lenses and found none. Napoleon, on the other side of the same table, examined his half of the room—standard procedure when breaking and entering an area as dangerous as a major Thrush base.

Finally, feeling as safe as they could in such a position, they stood up and set to work. Illya, the technician, produced a tiny camera and began snapping photographs of each drawing board, working methodically up one row and down the next. Napoleon, the instinctive hunter, began going through drawers.

Pencils, rulers, stacks of paper, jars of ink—nothing of value was to be found in that particular room. With a signal to Illya, he went to the door.

It was not locked, and the corridor was deserted. So far they had not seen a sign of any personnel since the two truant smokers had disappeared from the entrance to the tunnel. Either the place was severely understaffed, or everyone was attending compulsory lectures in the main hall. Or had been ordered to stay out of the area where two intruders were known to be. . . .

Nevertheless he took the chance and stepped out into the corridor. It looked like the one they had peeked into upstairs—apple-green, long, and lined with doors. But these doors had signs on them. Polylingual signs, with English on the second line. Napoleon's eye unconsciously selected his native language from the set and read it automatically.

DESIGN ENGINEERING was on five or six doors, each with different numbers and far enough apart to imply fairly large rooms behind them—probably equally as large as the drafting room they had landed in.

VEHICLE SYSTEMS was on the door to the room where Illya was busily taking pictures, and continued on other doors out of sight down the hall.

Across the corridor, sets of double doors led to an area called MATERIALS TESTING, and Napoleon followed his hunch.

Each door had a small panel of glass set about eye-level, and through this went a cautious look before the door was gently tried. It opened without complaint.

A huge barn-like room lay within, filled with all the massive and delicate impedimenta of a test area. He recognized strain gauges capable of pulling a steel bar in half, and others that would measure the stretch of a hair; shake-tables and vacuum chambers, ovens and cryogenic chambers sat about the floor—a torture chamber for the entire range of physical matter. Farther away other doors showed the CHEMICAL and ELECTRONIC divisions.

But time was short. Napoleon Solo returned to those traditional methods which have served spies well for centuries—he started going through the wastebaskets.

Wads of paper containing scribbled calculations went into his pack, as did memos in various languages, mimeographed bulletins and a letterpress instruction sheet, neatly imprinted with the Thrush letterhead. Then he moved on to a waste bin beside one of the testing devices.

It was empty. *Odd,* he thought, *that they should leave the wastebaskets full and clean out the remains of tested gear. Oh well, economy begins at home.* He moved on to the next bin—and the next. In the fourth he found something.

It was stuck to the side of the bin, and would have escaped a hurried inspection. Only the fact that it was dull in the soft light of the humming fluorescents caught his eye, and he started to reach for it when a bell chimed softly in the distance.

He straightened up suddenly as he heard footsteps in the corridor, and looked around for cover. As the steps stopped outside his door, he made his decision and jumped for the bin he had been examining. The box was quite large enough to hold him, and he peeled the thing off the side as he crouched there.

It was a scrap of plastic fabric, silvered on one side, and flexible. The shiny side had adhered to the side of the wastebin, and somehow been missed by the cleaning crew. But he didn't have time to look closely at it now—the door opened.

Quickly and quietly he pulled out his little transceiver and thumbed the transmission button. "Illya," he whispered, lips touching the microphone. "Chiggers, the cops!" A moment later there was a single, soft click, a wordless acknowledgment of receipt.

He tucked the little radio back in his inner pocket, and as an afterthought added the scrap of fabric. There were footsteps in the room now, and the hesitant sounds of a search. Then a voice broke the silence, harsh and metallic.

"This one is hiding in number twelve trash bin. The other one is behind the door in Vehicle Systems Drafting Room Four. Get those intruders. They've seen enough. But be careful—they're armed."

A fusillade of shots echoed from somewhere else—probably across the corridor. Illya would give a good account of himself. Not wanting to be left out or forgotten inadvertently, Napoleos selected his U.N.C.L.E. Special, since circumstances called for accuracy rather than circumspection, and stood up in his bin and began shooting, as coolly and accurately as on the target range. He dropped four rifle-equipped men before they had time to react to his presence, and then dropped himself back into the moderate protection of the sheet-steel box as their companions sent a hail of lead through the space where he had been standing. *So much for that gag,* he thought. *Now what'll we do for an encore?*

"You, in the bin," said the voice. "There are a dozen men with rifles pointed at you. You cannot escape. If necessary, we can place a small grenade in there with you, but the concussion could damage delicate equipment. You may have protection against tear gas, but we will try it first. On the other hand, if you wish to surrender, stand up slowly."

He heard no more shots from across the hall, and regretfully decided that a few minutes more of life was better than less. He stood up slowly, hands in the air.

"Take the pack," said the voice. "He has papers that should have been destroyed."

One of the gray-uniformed guards stepped forward, covered by his half-dozen fellows, and relieved Napoleon of the burden he bore. Glancing over their numbers, the U.N.C.L.E. agent allowed himself a slight smile. "I thought you said there were a dozen."

"If we had said half a dozen, you might not have surrendered. You Americans will fight great odds, but you are not suicidal," the concealed speaker answered him. "Now climb out of that bin and accompany your guards. We have a number of questions to ask you."

Chapter 12

"Head For Home, James!"

NAPOLEON OBEYED, handing his automatic over to the guard who extended a hand for it. "Take care of it," he said. "Every one of those I lose is paid for out of my salary."

With exaggerated care, the Thrush tucked the pistol into his belt and then beckoned to him. The rest of the group kept their rifles on point and maintained a distance of at least fifteen feet. Docilely Solo followed his guide to the door.

Outside he scanned the hall for a sign of Illya. If his partner was still free he could stage the usual daring last-minute rescue. And it began to look as if he would have to.

The door up the hall opened, and two guards came out, a limp figure with blacked face and a camouflage coverall slung between them. Napoleon sighed. So much for that approach to the situation. He began looking at the guards, sizing them up, and trying to figure the odds that Illya was bluffing and was actually ready to explode into action at the first hint of a fight. He looked critically at his partner, and decided it wasn't worth the risk. If he started something now, he might have to leave Illya behind—or carry him. Better to wait until he could carry himself.

He didn't have long to wait. One of the guards broke a capsule of something under the Russian's nose, and in a few seconds he was at least partly conscious. He was also under complete control.

Well, thought Solo, *here we are. Ten armed guards, and two of us. And there I stood with my rocket pistol.* At least they hadn't searched them thoroughly yet, and the Gyrojet still rested in the long holster in the small of his back. How could he get at it? Pretend to itch? And with only six rockets in the magazine, what about the other four guards? While he thought about it, Illya was pulled to his feet and shaken a few times until he looked able to stand and move about a little under direction. Then they were started off together.

After a minute or two of silence, Napoleon politely tried to start a conversation. "This is kind of awkward, isn't it?" he began. "I'll bet you don't have any really proper interrogation rooms set up here. You'll have to question us informally."

Nobody deigned to answer him. Illya shot him a

glance, then returned his silent gaze to the floor ahead of them.

But he continued. "Of course, the really awkward part will come when you try to explain how we got in here. Top security base, huh? Questions will be asked all the way up to the Ultimate Computer over this little business." He shook his head. "I wouldn't want to be in your shoes when responsibility for this gets shifted around. I'll bet the whole guard staff here gets purged." He chuckled affably. "About the best thing you could do for your own sakes would be to let us go and pretend it never happened. We sure aren't going to tell anybody."

The first guard finally spoke. "Easier just to kill you and drop bodies down vulcanole, *then* pretend it never happened."

Napoleon thought about this for a minute, then nodded thoughtfully. "Easier from *your* standpoint, perhaps," he said, "but what about ours?"

The guard didn't bother to say any more, and they marched into an elevator at the end of the hall. One of the Thrushes pushed a button and they started to rise.

Napoleon had been using the idle conversation as a cover for his increased rate of breathing. He was drawing air deeply into his lungs and using it to talk with while the additional oxygen filtered into his bloodstream. He was, in fact, hyperventilating—preparing his body for a period without breathing. Expecting that the offices to which they would be taken would not be on the same level, he had been looking forward to this elevator. Now it was up to Illya. His equipment had included the necessary. . . .

There was a subtle signal—a glance, accompanied by an almost imperceptible twitch of one eyelid and a slight wrinkling of the nose. None of the guards caught it.

The Russian's hand slipped casually to his belt, and fumbled briefly with something there. Napoleon took the cue, grabbed another lungful of air and held it. Since he was listening for it, he heard the faint hiss.

It was another twenty seconds before the elevator stopped and the door opened on another deserted hall. The two U.N.C.L.E. agents stepped over the slumped bodies of their guards, picking up a rifle each, retrieved their automatics, and looked up and down the corridor.

"All right," said Napoleon, after catching his breath, "you've got the sense of direction. Where did we come in?"

"The steel walls are interfering with my natural compass, but I think it's this way."

They ran. They were halfway to the end of the corridor when the loudspeakers came to life.

"All personnel," the voice resonated, "clear level two. Intruders at large. Secure all doors. Guards, converge on level two, corridor six. Observe caution—they are armed and extremely dangerous."

The first contingent of guards came running around a corner a short distance ahead of them, failing to observe the ordered caution. Two rifles set on fully automatic thundered in the echoing corridor, and the survivors fell back in disorder. Napoleon and Illya discarded their empty weapons and picked up fresh ones.

The loudspeakers rattled again. "Guards—load rounds of Alpha ammunition. Do not shoot to kill."

"Alpha?" asked Napoleon. "What's that?"

"I don't know about you," said Illya, "but I do not intend to wait around and find out. The local announcer said we were on level two. I'll bet the exit shaft we came in by opens off level one—top level."

"How do you know level one wouldn't be the bottom level?"

"Because we came up four levels in the elevator from where we were captured. You should pay more attention to things, Napoleon."

"All right. Where are the service stairs?"

"Over there. See the sign that says *stuparo*? That

means stairs. But the door is probably locked. Let's get back to the elevator."

"What makes you think it'll be working?"

"They have to get more men to our floor."

They pushed aside the sleeping guards, whose bodies had been left blocking the door open, and sniffed the air. The gas had already dissipated. They jumped in as the door slid closed and pushed the top button.

The loudspeaker was behind the times when they stepped out. "Seal level two," it said, a note of anger in the voice. "Corner them and capture them."

Napoleon and Illya smiled triumphantly at each other, and started up the corridor. After a couple of intersections, Illya suddenly turned right and pointed to a large pair of doors across the hall some hundred feet away. Each half had a glass panel in it, and a red sign above the door said something about unauthorized personnel keeping out. Napoleon pointed this out as they trotted towards it.

"Fine," said his partner. "If you want to go back and get a surface pass, you go right ahead. I won't wait for you."

"Under the circumstances, I guess we can probably get away with it just once. But I hope they won't consider it a black mark against our records."

"*I* hope they haven't sealed the door."

The loudspeaker brayed again, and its metallic voice was all around them. "Open level two," it barked. "They are making a break for surface passage Delta on level one."

"You guessed!" said Napoleon bitterly as they skidded to a stop at the doors, and found them immovable.

Illya shook his head and pulled something out of his pocket. "I think the time is past for subtlety," he said. "I'll blow it."

Napoleon fell back, shifting his attention to the hall behind them. He snapped the rifle's control over to semi-auto and pointed it down the corridor.

Seconds later a gray-helmeted head poked around the corner. The rifle spat flame, and the head disappeared. Part of the shoulder was still visible, however, and it fell to the floor. Napoleon hugged the wall, and pulled his stomach in as far as it would go.

A shot from a concealed marksman slapped into the door near him, and he pulled in a little further. Apparently they were only shooting wildly in hopes of connecting. He glanced at the impact spot and saw the remains of the bullet. It was only slightly damaged—a small hypodermic dart. That must be Alpha ammunition—probably some knockout juice. Not that it mattered much—if it connected, it might as well be a bullet as far as they were concerned. Better a bullet, in fact; with a slight wound he could keep going, but this would put him out of the fight entirely with only a scratch.

Illya called from behind him, "It's going! Down!" and he dropped flat, hands over his ears, feet towards the door, body limp.

The blast threw him a few feet and knocked all the wind out of him, and the concussion made his head ache—it was actually too loud to have been heard. At least it would discourage their attackers from coming around the corner for the next minute or two, and give them some head start up the tunnel.

Napoleon was on his feet again in a moment, and past the shattered ruin of the door a moment later with Illya hot behind him.

A faint glow of starlight scarcely warned them as they approached the end of the tunnel, but then there was a cool sea breeze in their faces, sloping lava under their feet, and a glittering sheet of stars across the whole sky above them. And then they were off, bounding downhill, careless of uneven ground and treacherous rocks.

Finally the protective shade of the forest was around them, and they slowed, panting for breath.

"Okay, trusted guide, you got us out of there. Now can you find where we left the scuba gear?"

"No trouble, *kemosabe*," said Illya. "Follow me."

It wasn't quite that easy. In a matter of five minutes feet could be heard crashing through the brush after them, and their progress to the beach was impeded from time to time by the necessity of pulling into a small invisible ball under a bush while the unfriendly natives went stomping past.

Between guard platoons they were able to work their way gradually downhill towards the sound of the surf, and eventually the trees parted before them and black sand spread down to the curling breakers, foam white under the stars.

Illya held out a restraining hand. "Let's follow under the trees," he said. "They probably have infrareds."

Napoleon nodded. "I *knew* there was something important we left home."

"Next time we'll remember. You can carry it instead of that rocket pistol."

They started down along the beach, paying attention to the woods on their right.

The stars near the eastern horizon were dimmer against a soft gray sky than they had been against the bottomless velvet of night when Illya stopped and pointed. "Over there somewhere," he said.

Flame spat out of the darkness of the trees, and a bullet snapped the air between them. They were flat on the ground by the time the sound reached them. Illya wriggled across the distance between them and whispered, "I was about to say, our gear is stowed over there."

"About where the other end of the target range is located?"

"Just about."

Napoleon sighed, and fished out his U.N.C.L.E. Special. "Now I know why they taught us to put these things together in the dark. Let's see—shoulder stock . . . silencer . . . flash shield. . . . The telescopic sight won't do any good here; I can't see him anyway. There we are." He rested his assembled weapon on his forearm, and directed it towards the trees. After a few seconds he said, "Come on, fella—shoot again so I'll know where you are."

But he didn't. Half a minute passed.

"Maybe he changed his mind," said Napoleon, consideringly. "Illya, old man, why don't you stand up and see?"

"If it's all the same to you," said his partner, "I'd rather wait as close to the ground as I can. Would it be all right if I just waved something?"

"Fine, but don't just lie there. My hand's getting tired."

It was another half minute before he heard an answer. "Here's a piece of driftwood with my shirt over it. Ready?"

"Any time you are."

Illya raised the stick cautiously. A rifle cracked in the brush and the shirt jumped. The U.N.C.L.E. Special coughed twice, and a listening silence returned to the jungle beach. The two intruders joined it in listening, and heard nothing. After a bit Illya raised the shirt again, and drew no response.

"Either you got him, and he'll be no further trouble, or you missed him and he's waiting for us to expose ourselves," said Illya helpfully.

"Okay—let's go see."

Napoleon gathered his feet under him, took a deep breath, and broke for the trees. He ran zig-zag, in a half-crouch, his automatic ready in his fist. No fire came at him, and then he was flat on the ground again, under cover. A few seconds later Illya joined him.

Together they crept cautiously through the sparse growth towards the spot where they had left their cache. Illya recognized the tree, and Napoleon spotted the gray-uniformed body lying a few feet away.

"Another point for our side," he said, checking the

Thrush over and clipping off an insignia. Section Three was always interested in details of Thrush uniforms.

Meanwhile, Illya was poking his stick into the soft earth, looking for their bundle. He found it quickly, and was brushing the dirt and loam off it when his partner returned.

The two slipped into the wet-suits and scuba gear quickly, and sealed their automatics back in the rubber pouches which would protect them from the highly corrosive sea water and the pressures at one hundred feet.

Then they were ready. Illya flipped on his pocket transceiver and sent the simply coded signal which would turn on the lights in their minisub, then tucked the silver cylinder in his pouch and sealed it. Then they headed into the surf.

Napoleon had set his mask over his face and taken the mouthpiece in his teeth when a spout of silver spray shot up a foot from him. Illya surface-dived in four feet of water and caught an out-going wave. Solo was right behind him.

Legs straight, kicking from the hips, the two men drove for deeper water. Somewhere out and down there was their only passage home. Solo had a wrist compass built into his suit, and by it he steered them through the inky water on a course due east. The depth gauge beside it crept downward—sixty feet . . . seventy feet . . . They hugged the coral-crusted bottom and squinted ahead for the lights of the sub.

Something bubbled faintly behind them, and he turned his head. A green glow filtered down along the slanting bottom, weaving as it approached. Napoleon snapped his fingers twice, and the muffled clicks caught his partner's attention. He gestured with his light, and saw Illya react as he saw the signs of their pursuers.

Napoleon directed his light at his free hand and began finger-spelling. *Go to sub. Wait five minutes.* Illya nodded and swam off down the slope again. In a moment he was lost in the darkness.

Napoleon snapped off the light and wriggled around, opening the zipper on the front of his suit and letting the sea water flow in around him, and found the lump tucked in his waistband. His secret weapon. He hadn't had a chance yet to use it with his unbelieving partner as witness, and it was a little frustrating. But the job came first, especially if it was a question of survival. Illya had the pictures, and he had the rocket pistol. And now was the time to use it.

He relaxed consciously, and slowed his breathing. No sense making a lot of bubbles that would attract the enemy's attention before it was inevitable, if indeed it was. The rocket pistol made very little flash underwater, and the direction of its bubble-exhaust would be practically impossible to trace under these conditions.

As the light approached, its green color grew more yellow and he could begin to see three swimming figures against and about it. He lay very still, holding to a clump of coral and steadying himself.

They were about thirty feet away as he pulled the cocking lever forward and down and raised the pistol.

The first shot made quite a roar for something so small. It sounded something like a torpedo being launched, as it was; and it had a similar effect on one of the swimmers—he stopped swimming and began thrashing about. If he had started bleeding immediately, his associates might have got an idea of what was happening. But the one with the light directed it at the bottom, scanning for a stingray or sea urchin which might have given the victim a dangerous sting. And while he was looking, he too was stung.

The light, released from his grip, drifted slowly down to rest on a branch of coral. The third Thrush looked about wildly, and saw a dark cloud beginning to ooze from the small tear in the suit of his friend. He couldn't have guessed what was attacking them, but he knew enough to head for the surface.

As the range opened, Napoleon's next two shots tore the water on either side of the fleeing diver, and his third was spent before reaching him. It was a split-second decision whether to follow him and prevent his alarm from getting to the land.

His knowledge of the abilities of their minisub made his decision for him. If they had scuba guards ready, Thrush must have reasoned that underwater would have been the only possible access to this island. Therefore, they would have a full-sized submarine which would probably be prowling the off-shore waters within minutes, whether their frogmen came back or not. And the U.N.C.L.E. sub could probably swim faster, dive deeper, stay down longer, and come up drier than anything Thrush could muster on such short notice. With his other hand he left the hammer-lever up gently.

He retrieved the dropped underwater light, and started back down the long slope into darkness.

It was less than a minute before the lights of the minisub began to be visible ahead of him. He extinguished the light he carried, and swam directly to the porthole and looked in.

There was Illya, lounging in the pilot's seat, feet up on the control panel, looking at his wristwatch. Napoleon tapped on the glass, and waved. Illya looked up and gestured over his shoulder towards the hatch. Napoleon nodded and swam up around the bulge of the hull to where the circle of white marked the entrance to the airlock.

Fifteen seconds later he was inside, and with practiced touch hit the buttons sealing the hatch and starting the electromagnetic pumps that replaced the sea water with air. He'd only been underwater some six or seven minutes—surface pressure would be safe for him.

Illya was still in the same position as Solo came out of the lock into the control sphere, but he spoke as the dripping suit slipped to the floor. "Steam is up, Captain. Fasten your seat belts and we'll be off."

"Excellent," said Napoleon, climbing into his contour couch and hooking the nylon straps about himself. "Head for home, James—it's been a long, tiring night!"

Section IV : "Is There No Way Of Stopping It?"

Chapter 13

"The Highest Con In The History of the World."

ALEXANDER WAVERLY leaned back in his chair and stared at the smoke rising from the other end of his pipe. He nodded slowly, as if considering something he didn't like. After some time he spoke, and his voice was tired.

"Of course it had to be Thrush. But none of our sources indicated they had any actual space potential beyond orbiting small single units. Something this large . . ."

A pneumatic tube coughed near his elbow and he reached for the message cylinder. A sheet of yellow paper was rolled up inside it. He unrolled it in silence and gave it a glance which committed every word to memory. He leaned forward and handed it across to Napoleon Solo.

"Report from Section Five," he said. "Complete analysis of that scrap of material you brought back with you."

Napoleon looked over the paper, and Illya read over his shoulder. "Hundred and fifty pounds per cubic foot, very high reflectivity, low tensile strength . . ."

"Seems kind of flimsy to build a spacesuit out of," said Illya.

"That's what Section Five thinks," said his partner. "Too thin, too light. No radiation protection at all. And the backing is not one that could be laminated onto a sturdier spacesuit—wouldn't be practical."

He stared at the report for a while, then set it resignedly on the table. Finally he looked up at Waverly. "So we can't do anything to the Monster Wheel anyway," he said. "We know where the base is. There were enough plans and other materials lying about to prove the Monster Wheel was launched from there. We could simply let the government know what we've found, and have a flight of bombers level the island."

Waverly shook his head slowly, and his face was worn. "They wouldn't be able to." He leaned forward and rested both hands on the table. "There is absolutely no reason to destroy that base. They have done nothing legally or morally wrong. The Monster Wheel has made no aggressive moves, and there is no law in the world against launching a space station without a license." He smiled slightly. "I seem to be repeating this statement twice a day."

"Are the voice broadcasts continuing?"

"Yes—regularly. Nothing new in the material, though. The view is always wonderful, the radiation level is quite acceptable, the life support systems are functioning perfectly, no trouble with micrometeorites. Nothing about observations of ground installations in any countries; nothing about solar fluctuations; nothing about any astrophysical observations. In short, nothing at all of value to us. And they still refuse to acknowledge any ground transmissions."

Napoleon Solo thought, and looked at his partner as he did so. A bell was ringing insistently somewhere in the back of his brain, reminding him of something he had seen but not noticed during those few busy hours inside the Thrush base on Dauringa Island. No—it was something he *hadn't* seen, and had not missed . . . until now.

And an idea began to grow in his mind—an idea so unbelievable, so completely unthinkable that it just might actually be true. Before it was fully formed he spoke to Illya. His voice was low and even, but it shook just slightly.

"Illya," he said, "you got a good look at a lot of material while you were taking pictures. Did you see anything there remotely relating to life support systems—water recycling, atmospheric maintenance, waste disposal, food supplies and preparation, or the like?" He paused briefly, then without waiting for an answer he continued. "For that matter, did you see anything in your travels resembling any interior plan of that space station?"

Illya's brows drew together and his eyes darkened slowly. He considered for several seconds before he answered. "I . . . don't think so. There were plans of all types for rocket vehicles, and a few sketches of the Wheel, and a number of circuit diagrams . . . and that's all I can remember."

Napoleon nodded, and his heart began to pound a little faster. He faced his superior squarely, and a slightly mad smile began to appear as he addressed him. "Mr. Waverly, does Rameses still insist that the Monster Wheel is actually Egyptian property?"

Waverly looked closely at his best agent, and said, "You have an idea, Mr. Solo." It was not a question, but an acknowledgment. "Yes, your Egyptian friend, under full interrogation, played back for us the directions he was given when he was sent after—ah—that navigator."

"Schneider," said Illya.

"Yes. Herr Schneider," said Waverly. "His commander told him that the matter of this particular rocket launching was of the utmost importance to both their national security and their rightful place among the nations of the world." He turned to his desk and began to rummage in some papers. "The transcript of the interrogation has apparently been filed somewhere. Does your idea require it?"

Napoleon shook his head slowly, and stopped smiling. "No, it doesn't. The only thing that remains to be known is the present state of Egypt's national treasury."

"Easily found. What are you looking for?"

"A very large recent withdrawal."

Illya made a slight sound, and Waverly turned back from his desk to face Napoleon. He turned very slowly and deliberately, and when he had completed the turn he rested his elbows on the table and leaned forward on them. Then he said, "Yesterday afternoon the African section reported that, from analysis of a number of rumors, they estimated a probability of eighty percent that a ship carrying a large but unspecified sum of gold bullion sailed from Port Said three days ago, destination unknown. The 'large but unspecified' was figured to be on the order of possibly one or two billion dollars."

"Billion?" said Illya softly.

"Billion," said Waverly.

The sort of reverent hush that always follows the mention of astronomically huge sums of money was broken by another cough of the pneumatic tube. The time its contents were handed to Illya.

"Section Five's reports on the circuit diagrams you photographed. Short-wave transmitters, receivers, frequency multipliers of various sorts."

"Nothing else?" asked the Russian. "No radar, no observation devices of any kind?"

"None."

"Well, Napoleon, what does this do to your theory?"

"Illya, it is positively necessary to it."

"Mr. Solo, perhaps you would like to expound your theory for our benefit. Frankly, I think I may be getting an idea of what you are driving at, and I must say I consider it to be highly improbable."

"But . . ."

"Its improbability is only outweighed," continued Waverly imperturbably, "by the greater improbability of Thrush actually being capable of building a real space station and selling it to Egypt."

"Wait," said Illya, a terrible idea dawning upon him. "That couldn't just be a balloon up there."

"Why," said Napoleon softly, "not?"

He went on: "Look. They simply could not have put up a real one. All our information says they didn't have the capability; there was no time to build it without being seen; there are no arrangements for any life support systems; and if Thrush had a real space station, they wouldn't sell it—they'd keep it! Now, when you have eliminated all which is impossible, then whatever remains, however improbable, must be the truth. Picture a balloon—like the Echo satellite, but shaped into a wheel the same way a Mickey Mouse balloon is made. It could have been launched in a single missle complete with a cylinder of compressed gas to inflate it to half a pound per square inch and a few hundred pounds of electronics gear." He was talking faster now as more pieces of the idea began falling into place.

"Even if they had the capability of constructing a full working space station, it couldn't have been put in orbit all at once. It would have to have been constructed there. Lots of ships would have had to go back and forth from the surface to the construction orbit, and it would have taken time. It couldn't possibly have avoided observation before it was finished. But did anyone even see the shuttle ships the crew was supposed to have been sent up on?

"The radio signals—all they prove is that there's a transmitter of some kind up there. A powerful one, probably powered by solar cells. The receivers could be coupled to recording tape units which could play back anything through the transmitter. And anything could be sent up from earth on a tight beam with some kind of coded signal, to start the recorders. The signals we thought were telemetry could have been handled the same way. Nobody has to be there—nothing has to be there but a shiny shell that looks like a space station from a distance of a thousand miles, and something to make noises that sound like a space station. *And that's all there really is!*"

Waverly nodded. "And they sold it to Egypt, probably promising their own crews occupancy on receipt of payment in cash. And that payment is on its way at this very moment."

"And Egypt has paid an incredible amount of gold for a bright, shiny balloon," said Illya slowly. "It's a con game. It's actualy all a confidence game."

"Yes," said Napoleon seriously. "The highest con in the history of the world. And what can we do about it?"

"If the Wheel cannot actually shoot back," said Illya, "it would be a simple matter to destroy it. There couldn't be any international recriminations—no nation has officially claimed it, and Egypt most certainly wouldn't once it was proved a fraud."

"There is only one flaw in that idea, Mr. Kuryakin," said Waverly. "This theory just might conceivably be wrong. And if we fired something at the Wheel, we would have about half an hour to contemplate the magnitude of our folly before thermonuclear missile reduced selected portions of the United States of America to a seething mass of radioactive slag."

Napoleon sat silent. After a pause Waverly continued thoughtfully: "No, I am afraid our only hope is to try to convince the Egyptians somehow to withhold payment. This will leave Thrush out by a fairly large investment. They will probably attempt to use the Wheel to threaten for a while, but eventually it will prove a toothless tiger.

"But we must move quickly. If Thrush collects this money, two billion could be sufficient to enable them to put up a *real* space station, actually capable of doing everything the Monster Wheel claims. And that Wheel, gentlemen, would not be sold to any national power. With it Thrush could—dare I say it—rule the world.

"Your job will be to stop that shipment of gold. We can find its current position and get you to it—I leave to you the mechanical problems of hijacking the ship. Meanwhile I will be working through diplomatic channels with the Egyptian government to justify your—ah—emergency activities.

"Will you be rested up and ready to leave again tomorrow morning? Probably a small twin-jet would be the best transportation."

"I think we can manage it. Illya?"

"Of course. Long vacations leave me bored."

"Very good. I think we shall also ship Rameses home now, full of the information we have garnered and well primed with your theory, Mr. Solo. His report may help convince the government there of the wisdom of following the course of action we advise."

"But the Wheel itself?"

"I shall present your case to our own government. In their position, I don't feel I would take the chance, but it is possible some method may be devised to test the defenses of the Wheel without bringing fire from the heavens down upon our heads. If such can be managed, it would probably serve to sway the Egyptian government where nothing else would."

"In the meantime?"

"We each have our jobs to do. Nothing can be done in the meantime except doing our best to shorten the meantime."

Napoleon and Illya looked at each other, and the Russian spoke first. "Well, I've never hijacked a shipload of gold before."

"When I was a boy," said Napoleon, "I wanted to be a pirate. And now here I am. Too bad we have to give it back afterwards. . . ."

Chapter 14

"We'll Have To Ditch!"

THE FIRST ANSWER came in before they left the next morning. Diplomatic communications with the Egyptian High Command had a net result of slightly less than zero—not only did they refuse to comment on the suggestion that the space station known as the Monster Wheel was of Egyptian origin, they were politely insulting about the very idea.

Waverly looked at the teletype flimsy he had been handed, and shook his head. Their sources within the governments of both the United States and Egypt would continue to work at getting the message through, but as long as the individuals responsible refused to admit their connection with the Wheel, they could not be approached with information as to its true nature.

He tossed the piece of yellow paper on his desk and reached for the intercom. "Is the airplane ready yet?"

"Fueling is almost completed, sir," came the answer. "Ready for takeoff in about twenty minutes."

"Very good. Put Mr. Solo on, please."

It was a minute or two before Napoleon answered. "Solo on, sir."

"Mr. Solo, it looks as if you will have your chance to play pirate. The Egyptian government has refused to look at our theories, and has denied hotly the existence of the ship you are being sent to stop."

"Well, if we pirate a nonexistent ship, we can't very well be hanged in chains, can we?"

"Your gibbets will be as unreal as the ship, Mr. Solo—no more so. You will be expected to exercise due care in your actions, and attempt to avoid the possibility of legal prosecution, which could reflect badly on both your government and your employer.

"The target ship has been located for us—its predicted coördinates will be transmitted to you by secure teletype in a few minutes. Have you decided upon a plan of approach yet?"

"We'd thought of flying over them and threatening to drop a bomb on them if they didn't heave to and surrender. Then we thought of anti-aircraft guns and shifted over to using a submarine and threatening to torpedo them if they didn't etcetera."

"Scarcely an original idea, Mr. Solo, but practical under most circumstances. Unfortunately, the target ship is an aircraft carrier of the Egyptian navy, and is equipped not only with anti-aircraft armament, but effective anti-submarine devices as well. I presume you have discarded your first two ideas?"

"If we hadn't before, we would now. But we came up with another old idea, which depends more on us personally than an open display of power would. It has the advantage that it is less likely to be answered with force. And we couldn't take on an aircraft carrier barehanded."

"It is a valuable attribute. Describe it."

"Well, the fact that the target is an aircraft carrier might affect the plan. . . . Hmm." There was silence on the other end of the circuit for a few seconds. "Yes, it does, but not much. How does this strike you, sir? We have a predated flight plan set up with NATO Air Control—you can arrange that—which takes us over the ship. Then . . ."

The windswept surface of the South Atlantic Ocean was a featureless blue forty thousand feet below the little twin-jet, and the sky was a lighter blue all about and above it. Only the quivering needles on the instrument panel indicated that the plane was actually moving at a fair fraction of the speed of sound. The two occupants of the pressurized cabin looked at each other and grinned.

The craft was equipped with only standard charts, and had no unusual electronic or navigational gear. Yet its passengers intended to find a single ship somewhere in the vast waste of water south of the Equator across sixty degrees of longitude—one twelfth of the surface of the earth.

The ship they were seeking had been spotted a day earlier, and they were now counting on the accuracy of their information to bring them together, with only an accurate compass and a chronometer. There are few radio beacons in this part of the world, and the seat of the pants has not been entirely supplanted by inertial guidance devices. But the course they were flying should cross the path of a certain officially nonexistent aircraft carrier shortly after 1600 GMT.

The whole plan they had devised back in New York hung on one single factor: the humanitarian instincts of the captain of that aircraft carrier. If he was coldly practical, they stood a good chance of never seeing land again. But if he had a shred of conscience and humanity, it could well be his downfall—and his country's salvation.

They would find out soon. Only some ten minutes separated their plane from the estimated position of their target. And it was time for the first step of the plan to go into effect. Napoleon nodded to his partner, who picked up the microphone of their air-to-ground radio, snapped the switch on the emergency channel, and began transmission.

"Mayday, mayday, mayday," he called. "Private aircraft Nan Eight-Zero-Three Love Jig calling Mayday. Developing fuel leak, and we will have to ditch in about ten minutes. Are there any ships in the vicinity?"

There was no answer. According to the last reports before their takeoff, there would be no ships within four hundred miles of this point—with one exception. The receiver hummed the mindless music of the ether, and no answering voice came with offers of hope for the crippled plane.

Illya called again. "Mayday, mayday, mayday. Private aircraft Nan Eight-Zero-Three Love Jig calling Mayday. We're losing fuel fast, and the engine may blow any minute. Is there anyone within range who can get help to us?"

This time there was an answer. It was faint, but it was clear, and it could only have come from one place. "Hello Nan Eight-Zero-Three Love Jig," it said. "What is your position? Over."

"This is Nan Eight-Zero-Three Love Jig. We're about twenty-one-thirty west, twelve degrees south. Who and where are you? Over."

"Correct your course to one-twenty and you should spot us in a minute or two. Can you steer? Can you glide? Over."

"Hello, life-saver. Yes, we can steer. Hydraulic system is still okay. Glide ratio is low, but we're at forty thousand feet. Coming about now to a course of one-twenty—one-two-zero—degrees."

During this conversation, Napoleon worked busily at the emergency lever which dumped the fuel in one of their tanks. The system would also allow a small amount of fuel to be squirted along the metal skin of the wing towards the port engine at the proper moment, giving the vivid impression of an engine on fire.

In another minute the highly volatile fuel had fallen safely from the jet and vaporized in the thin, cold air.

Illya was talking again. "Hello, unidentified station. If you're an aircraft carrier, we have visual contact. Shall we set down on your flight deck, or ditch? Over."

The answer to this was relatively unimportant. It would be nice to have the jet handy, and it would cost U.N.C.L.E. a fair sum to replace it, but the die had been cast when the ship had answered the distress call.

There was a pause of several seconds from the other station, then the voice said, "Can you handle a deck landing? If so, we'll have crash gear standing by for you. Over."

"Affirmative. Starting descent."

Illya replaced the microphone and gave the control wheel a gentle nudge. The little plane obediently began a descending spiral.

"He sounds like a nice guy," said Napoleon reflectively. "Almost a shame to pirate him. What say we don't make him walk the plank?"

"You're too soft-hearted to be a good pirate, Napoleon. Remember the cargo he's carrying and where it's going."

"All right, Captain Blood. But it's not *his* fault; he's only a tool of his government. In fact, I wouldn't be at all surprised if he's broken orders, either direct or implied, by saving our lives."

"Don't worry; when this is all over, he'll probably get a medal. We're at fifteen thousand feet—get ready with the engine fire."

"Ready."

"Then fire the nasty thing."

Napoleon twisted the red-knobbed lever and pushed it straight down. Almost at once a dull explosion sounded outside the left side of the plane, and the whole aircraft rocked violently. Illya fought with the control wheel for several seconds in a fierce attempt to keep from going into a tailspin, and cut the power to the starboard engine as soon as he had a hand free. Then he took a moment to glance out the window.

He smiled. "Beautiful," he said. "Just beautiful."

Napoleon could think of several things more beautiful. Outside the window their engine pod was a mass of roaring yellow and white flame which writhed along the surface of the wing, reaching for the almost-empty fuel tanks. Far away there was only a field of blue, alternating light and dark as the sky and the sea swept past. And the dark blue was getting closer at each pass.

Now it was showing texture, like a piece of fine cloth instead of glossy metal. And now the texture was expanding until the dancing specs of whitecaps whirled dizzily past as the jet continued to spiral downward. Illya was one of the few pilots in the world Napoleon would trust to do this to a plane he was in—it takes great control to appear to lose control completely, especially in front of the experts who were doubtlessly watching with critical and suspicious eyes from the deck of the Egyptian aircraft carrier below them.

Illya pulled out of the flat spin with a purposely clumsy

falling-leaf maneuver, and threw them into a reverse spin for a few seconds with only a couple hundred feet of very thin air between them and the jagged surface of the sea. Then he managed to level off.

Only one engine was functioning, and it was on half power. The other still roared flame, and the plane appeared, even to Napoleon, who knew better, to be limping badly.

The carrier was dead ahead of them, and growing slowly. Illya pulled the wheel hard back; and the jet climbed to the edge of a stall before he let it off. The maneuver gained them another hundred feet, and a clearer view of the ship.

It was an old carrier, of a type nearly made extinct by the attack on Pearl Harbor. The flight deck was short by modern standards, and the island large and awkwardly placed for a plane with the landing speed of the U.N.C.L.E. jet. But Illya throttled back until their air speed barely sustained them in flight, and started down the glide path.

There was a speck in a bright orange suit standing just below the near edge of the deck, and his arms waved frantically as they approached. Illya corrected his angle slightly, then more. Port wing still too low. He pulled at the wheel and kicked the right pedal to maintain the exact direction, and then the deck was leaping up at them. He pulled the nose up violently and cut the power to both engines as the leading end of the deck whipped under them.

There was just a moment of weightlessness, and then Napoleon's chair tried to slam the base of his spine through the top of his head, and almost succeeded. They bounced several times, and canted several degrees to one side. And then all was still, except for the sound of the turbines as their penetrating whine wound down the long chromatic scale towards silence.

Illya was the first to get his seat-straps unfastened and kick the door open, but Napoleon was close behind him. Figures were running across the deck towards them and their plane, and they ran away from it. Theoretically, it could be about to explode, and these sailors were risking their lives to extinguish the fire before it did any more damage to the plane or to their ship.

A foam wagon screeched up and began squirting detergent-laden spray over the blazing engine, and the flames vanished in seconds. A crew in asbestos suits hurried in and began checking to make sure the blaze was safely extinguished.

As they stood in their sweat-stained flight suits, Napoleon and Illya heard footsteps behind them even as the fire was brought under control. They turned to see a short, bearded man in a blue uniform with ranks of gold braid on the sleeves, who addressed them in English.

"Your plane may not be severely damaged," he said, "but I must tell you that you have by accident fallen into a very . . . embarrassing situation. We are on a mission of extreme secrecy, and you must stay as prisoners for some time. You will be well treated, but you cannot be allowed any contact with the outside world for a few weeks, perhaps less. I am deeply sorry, gentlemen—consider that a comfortable prison for two weeks is better than a watery grave for eternity." He spread his arms, and four armed guards stepped smartly forward.

"Do not think badly of me," he said. "You will soon be free, possibly with your jet repaired in our shops on board, and allowed to continue your flight to Yaoundé in Cameroon."

They looked surprised and he nodded. "Yes, I checked you out before I decided to save your lives. I am entrusted with this ship, and our mission is one which might attract spies or agents of foreign powers. But since your flight plan was perfectly plain and had been filed a week ago, before we ourselves knew our assignment, you could not have been here but by unhappy coincidence."

He turned and started towards a hatch. "Come," he

said. "You cannot even be allowed the freedom of the ship, for some days yet."

The guards bracketed them, and the two U.N.C.L.E. agents proceeded to follow the Captain of the treasure ship down companionways and passages deep into her steel heart.

Chapter 15

"Accidental Misfire."

ALEXANDER WAVERLY leaned back from the communications console and set his unlit pipe in an ashtray. His face looked tired, but his eyes were hard. Fifty hours had passed since his two top agents had disappeared into the South Atlantic, and not a word had been heard from them since their jet had gone down in flames. He had no choice now but to believe they were dead.

He felt no grief—he had sent too many men to their deaths in the line of duty to feel any more than a cold anger which he buried and directed at the enemy who made this constant cost necessary. A man in his position could afford to have few friends, and none within his own organization. He remembered Napoleon Solo only a few days before envying his desk job, and a thin, bitter smile creased the corners of his mouth. It was so easy to die . . . but others must live to carry through the job.

There was still a chance that either or both of them might still be alive, but hope had no place in an all-or-nothing game. When you were risking the lives of a billion people and the safety of the entire world, you played only on sure things.

But what did you do when there were no more sure things? It took a gambler's cool courage and evaluation of odds when the human chips were down to know the winning cards, bluff, bet and play, and still rake in the pot.

Napoleon Solo had possessed this talent to an extent his partner, for all his intelligence and technical capacity, could never attain. His instinctive ability to slip through the smallest loophole in Fate's contract had brought him back from disaster and worse time and time again. Waverly hoped for the sake of the organization—*his* organization—that it would this time. But now there was no way of knowing, and the odds were dropping.

No computer could have told when the odds shifted to favor the alternate attack. But Waverly was always a percentage player—almost always. And now the time had come to split the bet, call the bluff, and wait for the last card to fall. And if the other player really held the winning hand, to pay the score without regret.

He tapped a button on the communication console and said, "Get me a secure line to NASA headquarters in Washington. Doctor MacTeague."

It was perhaps thirty seconds or so before the crisp voice answered. Waverly spoke in cold, precise tones, describing their findings and their theory as to the nature and origin of the Monster Wheel. MacTeague had been appraised second-hand and in no detail; it was necessary that every fact be laid before him now.

Waverly set them forth in short, crisp sentences. When he finished, he said, "Doctor, a few days ago it was decided we could not risk a direct attack on the Wheel. Now I must report that in my opinion it is the only possible course remaining open to us."

MacTeague was not a professional bureaucrat; his position depended not on votes but on his performance and his efficiency. He took only a moment to say, "All right, Waverly. You know the situation and I don't. But I must insist on some kind of an out for us. You yourself admit the possibility that they might not be bluffing. It may be a small one, but we have to reduce the danger of retaliation. Remember, more than one hundred million lives hang in the balance."

Waverly nodded. "I am aware of the stakes, Doctor. And you are aware there is very little time left to resolve the situation. If that payment is made successfully, it will be only a matter of time until there is an actual Monster Wheel capable of all this Wheel has threatened. Admittedly the United States of America is being risked, but the stake includes the safety of the entire world. And if we refuse to take the chance, we will almost certainly lose by default."

"I'm sorry, Waverly. I really think I do understand the full situation. But my first responsibility is to the people of this country. Unless you can give me some additional factor in our favor, I cannot allow a missile to be launched at the Wheel." He paused. "I'll grant this: I will order a test probe capable of carrying a thermonuclear device prepared for a launch. It will be ready when—and if—you can find a way of bettering our odds. Right now all we have is a theory on which, frankly, I would be willing to risk my own life—but not the lives of a hundred million citizens."

Waverly said something to acknowledge, and pressed the disconnect button. He sighed deeply and leaned back in the chair. Absently he picked up his cold pipe and puffed at it for several seconds before realizing that it was still unlit. He stared at it vaguely, then set it down and leaned his head on the back of the chair and stared at the light metal ceiling.

Almost a quarter of the way around the world Napoleon Solo lay on a bunk and also contemplated a metal ceiling. The bunk was comfortable, the room was air-conditioned, the food was fairly good and regular. Personally, he had no complaints—unlike his partner, who was currently standing near the middle of the room, his head turning uncertainly from side to side.

"They don't have the room bugged, Illya. I'm sure of

it. Now stop worrying. They would have no earthly reason to plant a bug in the first mate's cabin, and no time to rig a good one in the few minutes they had before we were booked into it."

"All right. Besides, if it is bugged, we've probably given ourselves away by this time."

"Be honest—what you mean is *I* have given us away. And since we've gotten no reaction from anywhere it becomes increasingly obvious that I haven't. So stop worrying and relax."

Illya looked down on the American. "You look so relaxed it bothers me. What do you have up your sleeve?"

"Absolutely nothing but my trusty right arm, old friend. They've taken everything away from us but the clothes on our backs."

"They haven't taken our shoes, or the contents thereof—we could walk out of here anytime we wanted to."

"And where would we go? The ship is still all at sea, and so are we. We may be superhuman, but there are an awful lot of men on an aircraft carrier, even one this small. And since I haven't eaten my spinach today, I don't quite feel up to taking it over and turning it around single-handed."

"Not single-handed," said Illya. "After all, you've got me."

"All right," said Napoleon reasonably. "Double-handed, then. Even with my faithful Russian companion it's more of a job than I feel up to at the moment." He tapped at his chest and coughed experimentally. "Now maybe in another day or two I'll feel better. Sea air often does wonders for my constitution. When we get to wherever we're going, then you and I will have someplace to jump to if the going gets rough. Besides, our assignment was essentially to interrupt the transaction before the bird people flew away with the goodies. Wouldn't it be more fun to snatch them from their very claws?"

"And wouldn't you feel foolish if we missed?"

Napoleon shrugged, which was not easy while lying on his back. "There's nothing we can do now," he insisted. "We'll wait until there is." And as far as he was concerned, the subject was closed.

The Florida sun was touching the horizon behind them as they passed the armed guard at the door of the blockhouse and the heat of the day that had just ended radiated back at them from the concrete block walls. Alexander Waverly removed his hat and passed a handkerchief across his moist forehead as the steel door closed behind them. A mechanical voice somewhere said, "X minus two hours and counting."

Doctor MacTeague found a pair of padded chairs with a reasonably unobstructed view of the control area and lowered himself into one. "The broadcast has been prepared," he said. "The range safety officer will send it off about thirty seconds after the course correction has been made for a collision orbit. It'll be broadcast on the same frequency the Wheel uses to talk to the ground, as well as on the International Distress frequency and a half a dozen other reasonable frequencies, including the one that carries the world standard time signals from Greenwich. If there's anyone on board that Wheel listening they'll hear it."

Waverly took the other chair while MacTeague talked. Now he said, "How long will the total orbit take from launch?"

"About half an hour. The correction will take place about plus seven minutes. Have you heard anything from those two agents of yours?"

"No. It's been four days. The one piece of aerial reconnaissance we dared do showed the ship this morning still on course, approaching the island of San Juan de la Trine, about seven hundred miles south of the Cape of Good Hope. It looks as if this missile is our last hope."

"I wish it was a sturdier one." MacTeague sighed,

and shook his head. "If you're wrong about this, and they're not bluffing . . ."

"I am quite aware," said Waverly tiredly. "I will be responsible for the destruction of the United States of America."

"I don't suppose the responsibility really matters so much," said MacTeague. "If you're right, they will never know. And if you're wrong, there will be no one left to assign responsibility anywhere—let alone in a position to know what really happened. If that's any comfort."

"Not especially," said Waverly, and lapsed into silence. The decision had been made and implemented—the only decision possible under the circumstances. And now it simply had to be waited out. He fumbled for his pipe and tobacco, and began fitting one into the other.

It was dark outside the porthole, and only a single light burned in the comfortably furnished cell containing the two U.N.C.L.E. agents. There in semi-darkness, both minds were working vigorously.

"Did you once write, 'A poet can survive anything but a misprint'?"

Napoleon thought a moment and said, "No, I'm not Oscar Wilde. And it's *everything*, not *anything*."

With time weighing on their hands, they had returned to their game of Botticelli. At the moment Illya had two and Napoleon was currently defending, with a "W."

Illya lay back with his feet up and thought. Solo had a strong predilection for American poets, but so far only the literary field had been established by his free questions, so he was unrestricted in the nationalities he chose. "Did you write '*Jacques Bouchard*'?"

Silence followed. There is a lot of silence in the game of Botticelli, either preparing questions or searching for answers. Napoleon finally decided he didn't have this answer and said so.

"Pierre Wolff," said Illya. "You should pay more attention to the European theater. Now: Are you an American?"

"Yes."

"Thought so. In that case . . ." He went back to his mental file of American writers and was leafing slowly through it when the ship's engines stopped.

Both sat up. The faint distant throbbing had surrounded them for three days, until they were no longer aware of its presence. Then suddenly they were aware of its absence.

Napoleon spoke first. "Well," he said. "We seem to have arrived."

Illya rolled to his feet. "Fine. *Now* do we take over the ship?"

The American held up a restraining hand. "Not so fast, you mad impetuous Russian. There are many factors to consider. After all, it will take some time to unload all the cargo we think is here—unless they're throwing the ship and crew into the bargain . . ." He stopped short, and a thoughtful look darkened his face.

Illya smiled. "You hadn't thought of that, had you? They might not even bother to unload the gold. This is a good place to store it."

"And it's a good place to hijack it from. No, I think they'll put it in a secret cavern somewhere." He got up and went to the porthole, cupping his hands around his face and peering out into the night. "I wish I could tell where we are."

"No street signs visible?"

"Not even any lights. For all I know we may have stopped in mid-ocean, to transfer the cargo to a submarine."

"Or a dozen submarines. That much cargo is a lot of volume as well as a lot of weight."

"Wait a minute. There's something. Turn out that light, will you? Thanks." He looked long through the small porthole, then spoke again, and a deeply satisfied note was in his voice. "All is very well. There *is* an island out there, and we're lying to about a quarter mile from shore. I can see some buildings on the island—there's a moon. And I think I see what we were hoping for. There's something that looks like a radome on top of a hill maybe half a mile up from the beach." He stepped away from the window. "Come on and take a look. Our goal is in sight."

"Somehow," said Illya, "every time you say that it means we're in for a fight." But he came and looked, and eventually nodded. "It's a radome. Probably where they broadcast the signals to the Wheel."

"I wish we had our communicators."

"And I wish we had our guns. I also wish we had a batallion of Cossacks and a few tanks."

"I doubt if the Captain could supply us with those, but he has our radios—and our guns. And my cigarettes, come to think of it."

"So we walk up to him, explain the situation, and ask for them back?"

"No," said Napoleon regretfully. "He strikes me as the kind of man who would obey orders no matter how ridiculous they seemed. We'll just have to take them by force—or by stealth."

Illya expressed resignation. "Lead the way," he said.

As the moment approached for the launching, an air of tension quite out of proportion to the size of the firing grew in the quiet dimness of the control center. Every man there knew the actual mission of the missile on Pad Four. They had been briefed after the door was sealed.

On one monitor speaker the familiar voice of the Wheel droned in Esperanto about the beauties of outer space. The tracking station at Johannesburg had begun relaying the signal as soon as the satellite had cleared the horizon there.

The local controller's voice was steady over the loudspeakers as the last minute was ticked off by the hundreds of synchronized clocks inside the control system.

When the time came, only the faintest vibration was felt inside the building. On television screens the missile was surrounded by a cloud of smoke, and then it stood like a spike from the boiling clouds. It grew on a stalk of flame from the blasted earth, gathering speed until it pulled its taproot up after it and vaulted into the sky and was gone. Only a radar trace showed its path.

Attention shifted to a plotting board. The Monster Wheel was there, in its orbit safely away from the path of the short red line of grease pencil which already had a visible extension southeast of the peninsula of Florida on the map.

And the voice started counting again. "Coming up on minus five minutes to course correction. Mark. Minus five minutes."

Waverly found that his pipe had gone out, and the bitter taste of cold, used tobacco crept up the stem into his mouth. He grimaced, and spat into a wastepaper basket. He glanced at his companion, who reclined in his chair without a sign of tension—except where his hands gripped the arms. Waverly smiled slightly to himself, and started to clean the pipe.

"Course correction minus four minutes."

One of the detonators from the hollow heel of his shoe had opened the first door that stood between Napoleon Solo and freedom. The sound it made was not loud, and as hoped the crewmen were not thronging in the corridors. "Probably all up on deck," he whispered to Illya as they crept out and started for the Captain's cabin.

It was not difficult to find—they had been taken there for dinner shortly after their crash, and there had been relieved of all their possessions and had watched them being locked in the safe. They had received in return the Captain's assurance that the goods would be safely restored once this mission was completed and they could be sent on their way.

The Captain was probably on deck with his crew, supervising the unloading of his precious cargo. His door did not require the expenditure of another detonator, but the safe door did.

"Shameful security they have on this ship," said Illya disapprovingly as they blew the safe. "We should probably write them a letter about it when we get home."

"I wouldn't," said Napoleon. "We may need to do this again sometime, and I would rather it was easy."

"That's the trouble with you," said Illya. "You're soft."

There was a sharp sizzling sound and a *whap!* like two padded boards being slapped together as the charge went off. A bit of smoke dissipated quickly and revealed the safe door hanging by one hinge.

"Sloppy," said Illya.

Napoleon shook his head. "You're just full of criticism tonight," he said. "Right now we're in a hurry.

"We could have taken ten or twenty minutes to feel out the combination," he continued as he began to rifle the safe, "and risked being walked in on if the Old Man wanted a drink. *That* would have taken some fast explaining. Our absence won't remain a secret very long anyway, and I'd much rather . . . Ah! Here we are. He is, at least, an honest man." He tossed Illya his automatic, and pocketed his own U.N.C.L.E. Special and the Gyrojet that had saved his life twice so far. He handed Illya one of the communicators and kept the other, then snapped open his cigarette case. "Bless his little heart," he said as he checked the contents. "They're all here."

"I'm sure his mother would be proud of him," said Illya. "Now that we have the radios, shouldn't we check in? We've been out of touch for three days, and they might start to worry."

"We can wait a little longer. Mr. Waverly has more things to worry about than us. Besides, if we did call him, he'd only say, 'Well, Mr. Solo, do you have that job done yet?' and we'd have to tell him we don't. And I'd be ashamed to do that after three days. So let's go finish the job . . ."

". . . And then we'll call him," said Illya. "All right. After three days another few hours won't matter."

"It's not irrevocable, Waverly," said Dr. MacTeague. "You can still have it stopped."

"My orders are not valid here," said Waverly. "*You* can have it stopped."

"I will not do so unless you recommend it."

"Then, my dear sir, it will not be done," said Waverly with cold finality.

And they sat and listened together as the last seconds trickled away in metallic clatterings of the loudspeaker.

"Five . . . four . . . three . . . two . . . one . . .

"Zero! Course correction implemented." Pause. "Radar check reports correction accurate. Collision minus approximately twenty-two minutes."

"Ready with radio transmission," said another voice. There was a wait of almost a minute, and then the voice said, "Calling Space Station One. Calling Space Station One. This is Cape Kennedy Control. We have had an accidental misfire, and a small missile has left its planned orbit. The ground destruct mechanisms have failed to operate. It will approach your orbit in twenty minutes, forty-five seconds. Coördinates relative your position three-twenty degrees polar, azimuth minus fifty degrees, plus-minus five degrees on both. This is not a hostile missile. It is an accidental misfire. Destroy the missile. Repeat—destroy the missile."

The voice of the Wheel chattered on inanely, as the message began to repeat.

MacTeague and Waverly looked at each other in the cool darkness of the control center.

"Now," said MacTeague, "it *is* irrevocable."

Chapter 16

"Dauringa Island Calling The World!"

FLOODLIGHTS SPARKLED on the surface of the ocean on the landward side of the ship, and voices shouted back and forth from the deck to small boats which bobbed on the night-black water.

The seaward side was unlit, unwatched, and nearly deserted. The control tower which rose from the starboard side of the flight deck cast a broad dark shadow across the midnight sea. And within that shadow two men quietly lowered a convenient lifeboat. The davits were well-lubricated, and not a sound betrayed them. In a matter of minutes they were free of the ship and pulling their oars in the direction of the open sea.

It was some time before they were far enough away from the ship to turn; then they rowed parallel with the shore for almost half a mile. The illuminated area was large, and their success was of greater importance than the few minutes which could be save by a more direct course.

They had been rowing with only the stars and the distant lights from the ship to guide them for almost an hour before Napoleon whispered, "Up oars!" In the silence that followed, he could hear clearly the hiss and rumble of breakers behind him. Beaching a small boat through surf is a great deal more difficult than swimming through it in scuba gear, and neither their guns nor their other gear was waterproof.

He shipped his oars and turned in his bow seat to face ahead, then whispered over his shoulder to Illya, "We're coming up on the surf. Get set for a few strokes with all your weight when I give the word."

His partner grunted acknowledgment, and Napoleon opened his eyes wide, reaching through the darkness for the frothing lines of white that would mark the shore.

The soft repeating hiss grew as they neared the beach, and then he could see the foam. The little boat rocked violently as a wave rose up and swept under them, and Napoleon said, "Now! Hit it!"

Illya hit it—three powerful strokes with the oars that drove them along the trough of the following wave. The water rose as the wave overtook them, lifting them up as he shipped the oars and grabbed the gunwales, and then, with a swoop like a high-speed elevator, leveled itself out upon the sand with a muffled roar, sank away in a welter of white suds, and was gone.

Napoleon leaped out of the boat and grabbed the bow. "Come on," he said. "We've got to get this under cover."

Together they dragged the boat up the narrow hard-packed beach and into the shelter of the first row of vegetation. Then they crouched in the shadows for several minutes listening for any evidence of their detection.

Finally Illya spoke softly. "So much for *their* security systems," he said. "Napoleon, do you realize how many times we have breached Thrush's walls in the last few weeks?"

"Yes," said Solo. "Approximately twice. And if you will remember, it hasn't been exactly easy either time. Would you feel better if they caught us?"

"Well, no. But I wouldn't be so worried. There *ought* to be guards patrolling the island."

"Why? Nobody could get here without being detected."

"Unless they came underwater, like we did on Dauringa. And I imagine they'll be taking steps to prevent that, now, too. And in addition I still expect some kind of beach patrol."

"So do you want to wait for them?" asked Napoleon. "Let's move inland."

They navigated across the island by the stars, keeping

the Southern Cross ahead of them and slightly to their right. They had been under way for almost an hour, proceeding with all caution, when the crest of a rocky hill fell away in front of them and they saw their destination on the next peak, less than half a mile off.

It squatted like a great white puffball fungus, pale against the ocean horizon in the light of the southern stars. Faint lights shone here and there through openings about the building at its base, and other small buildings clustered nearby as if seeking protection.

Beyond and to the right, down a short, precipitous canyon, a small patch of beach could be seen, where lights were strung about with a carnival air. And out to sea the aircraft carrier was likewise illuminated—a floating island of light in the vast lonely darkness of the South Atlantic Ocean.

"Looks like a festival," said Illya.

"It is," said Napoleon. "The colorful natives of . . . what is this island, anyway? . . . are celebrating the arrival of the ship which bears all that their simple hearts could desire."

"Yes. Two billion dollars in gold."

"Well, that would be all *my* simple heart could desire."

"You have a point, Napoleon." He smiled slightly. "I wonder if the celebration will extend to drinking themselves into a stupor?"

"It would be handy," Solo agreed, "but knowing Thrush I'm inclined to doubt it. There are only certain specifically designated times when one may drink oneself into a stupor, and they do not include the moment when the biggest con game in the history of the world is in the process of paying off. But don't let it worry you—if the two of us can't take on a whole flock of Thrushes without getting them stinkered first, it's time we turned in our Hero badges and left the game."

"Now, Napoleon, I didn't say it was *necessary*, I just said it would be *convenient*. Besides, as long as our luck holds, we can slip in there, plant our little mementos, and slip out again. Then while Thrush is fluttering its feathers we sneak back on board the ship, take the Captain at gunpoint, tell him our whole story, and suggest he contact his headquarters."

"Very good, Illya. You remember the plan I outlined for you last night."

"Quite well. I also remember you didn't say anything about how we get back to the ship, how we capture the Captain, or how we convince him not to order us shot as soon as our gun hands get tired."

"Oh, we'll work that out when the time comes. I always like to leave myself room enough to play around with a plan to suit the situation. Flexibility is the keyword, my boy—flexibility."

"Spare me the lecture. We have some flexing to do right now. With only enough high-explosive here for a couple of those buildings, which ones do we hit?"

"Search me. Let's go take a look while the colorful natives are all down at the dock welcoming the tourists."

Illya shook his head. "Security," he said. "Shameful."

Apparently the natives were indeed all down at the docks. The two U.N.C.L.E. agents found themselves in the shadow of the big radome without so much as a sound from a guard. They had met one guard, but he had hardly had time to make any sound, except for a soft thump as his body hit the ground. And he seemed to have been alone. At any rate, they were here, and unchallenged.

They peered in the window of one of the side buildings, and saw the squatting, buzzing bulks of a pair of sturdy electrical generators, both in operation. A good target for destruction, if they could find no others—but it would be better to cost Thrush as much technical equipment as possible, and generators were easily replaced.

Then they came to the base of the bulging white dome, and to a window in its base construction. They peered in, and up.

A single unshielded light bulb cast a distorted shadow on the inside of the heavy fabric—an intricate shadow of the steel and wire gridwork of a gigantic directional antenna which at the moment was pointed almost directly overhead. But even as they watched it tilted ever so slowly towards the north, as slowly as the minute hand of a clock, or slower.

It took Napoleon a moment to realize what it was. "It's tracking the Monster Wheel," he whispered. "Probably sending up whatever the crew is supposed to be saying for the next eighteen hours."

Illya nodded. "And the whole world will be hearing it. What a shame it can't tell the world it is a hoax."

Napoleon looked at his partner, and a deep and satisfied smile began to spread slowly over his face. "Illya," he said, "you may just have something there. Let's check these other buildings."

One was filled with bunks, all presently unoccupied. But the next was full of ranks of electronic gear, most of it readily recognizable. It included three tape decks, two running at different speeds.

The door was locked, but not seriously; they were inside in a matter of moments. It was Illya who spotted an acetate-sheathed sheet of typing headed EMERGENCY BROADCAST PROCEDURES, but it was Napoleon who located the cabinet where a microphone waited.

"You know," he said, "this is even more fun than hijacking a shipload of gold."

"It may be for you," said the Russian, eyeing the microphone uneasily, "but personally I always get nervous with these things."

"This is not time to get mike fright. You'll have to broadcast in the languages I don't know. Look, I'll go on first, and all you have to do is translate what I say. Then we'll plant our bombs and get out of here."

He scanned the instruction sheet, and quickly made the necessary adjustments. Now it took only the flick of a switch and the touch of a button to replace the recorded voice now coming from the Monster Wheel with their own voices, admittedly coming from the Earth. He paused. "Say, did we ever figure out what island this is?"

Illya shook his head.

Napoleon shrugged. "Okay, I'll identify us as Dauringa Island, then. When Egypt discovers they've been conned, they may decide to use an officially uninhabited island for bombing practice, and I'd prefer it to be one I wasn't on."

He took a deep breath, flicked the switch and pushed the button. The voice coming out of the speaker stopped in the middle of a word, and was replaced by a whistle of feedback that grew rapidly in intensity until he found the knob to kill the monitor. Then he spoke, and saw the needle on the VU meter dancing across the dial.

"Hello, hello," he began tentatively. "This is Dauringa Island, calling the world. Dauringa Island, calling the world."

In a dimly lit room at Cape Kennedy, Alexander Waverly sat up in his chair and listened. An unpleasant electronic shriek had just come out of the speaker which was monitoring the transmission from the Monster Wheel, and then, after a moment's silence, it was replaced by a familiar voice.

"Hello," it said. "Hello. This is Dauringa Island, calling the world."

Waverly leaned back in his chair, and his face folded up on itself in his finest and deepest smile in three weeks. Solo had come through.

The voice continued: "The supposed space station called the Monster Wheel is a hoax. It is nothing more than a gigantic balloon with a radio inside, broadcasting threats which are as empty as itself. Soon it will be destroyed, as final disproof of its claims of strength. Those who were taken in by it are warned to be more careful in the future."

Alexander Waverly leaned back in his chair in the cool

dimness of the blockhouse, and surrounded himself with a cloud of aromatic blue pipesmoke, as Illya's voice took over, repeating the message in Russian. Not only complete success in pricking the balloon of threats, but with timing that could not have been better arranged if every step had been centrally cöordinated. Napoleon's voice returned in French, followed again by Illya, this time in Chinese. The flashing lights of the automatic sequencer display on the control console across the blockhouse were flashing off the last minute as Napoleon spoke in German and Illya's voice finished the final statement in the language affected by the Monster Wheel itself.

". . . *esti pli zorga estonte,*" he concluded, and the carrier wave continued its unmodulated hum for perhaps thirty seconds while the lighted numbers supplied the countdown. As they crossed zero, it simply ceased.

And it was as simple as that, as far as the world was concerned.

Somewhere in the star-crusted, black-floored vault a thousand miles above the night side of the Earth, a metal cylinder had flashed towards a slowly-turning wheel and exploded into a shower of steel shards, each of which continued moving, faster than a rifle bullet relative to the target.

In a fraction of a second, the thin fabric was a tattered rag. The small package of electronic equipment at the hub was punctured three times, and the solar power panels, inoperative in the Earth's shadow, were shattered to powder. A thin cloud of Argon gas puffed out invisibly, and began to disperse as the random motion of its atoms sent them in every direction towards the edges of the universe.

No human eye saw its ending. Only a few radar traces showed any change as the rigid wheel collapsed slightly and began to drift from its orbit as it absorbed a fraction of the kinetic energy of the shrapnel that had pierced it. And a few receiving sets noted the cessation of the signal from the ruined transmitter.

Napoleon and Illya were a few hundred feet above the Thrush island base in a stolen helicopter when the first of their time fuses completed its job and the radome blossomed out in a billow of yellow flame. Within seconds one of the adjoining buildings on the hilltop disappeared in a similar blast, silent for several seconds at their distance. Before the sound of the two explosions reached them they were able to see the light metal structure of the big antenna sagging and crumpling in raging flames as its protective umbrella floated earthward around it.

"Now," said Napoleon, "there will probably be a whole swarm of hornets raging over the island since we set fire to their nest. And obviously the only thing for us to do is go back to the ship."

"Try to sneak back into our comfortable cell and pretend we haven't been outside all evening?"

"I'm afraid not this late. *Toujours l'audace*, Illya. I think we should continue with our original plan."

"Well, as long as we're heading towards certain death, you won't mind if I check in at home."

"Not at all."

Alexander Waverly was startled slightly when his communications unit signaled him. Nothing less than a Code Seven call should reach him here. He answered, and heard a familiar cool voice murmur from the speaker.

"Agents Kuryakin and Solo reporting in, sir. The voice of the Wheel has been silenced, and we are on our way back to the ship for the gold. You may feel free to destroy the Wheel at your leisure."

The U.N.C.L.E. Chief felt a wave of relief wash over him—not only because he had been saved the time and expense of training two new top agents. But there was no emotion in his voice as he said, "Very good, Mr.

Kuryakin. The Wheel has already been destroyed, for that matter, shortly after you gentlemen completed your lecture. If you had been a few minutes later in your broadcast, it would have passed entirely unheard. Will you need any help in securing the ship?"

"Despite my partner's characteristic confidence, sir," came the voice from the far South Atlantic, "I feel some help could definitely be useful. If you could attempt to contact the Egyptian High Command, and have them transmit orders to the Captain of the ship that he coöperate with us, we would have a much better chance of defending the vessel against the forces of Thrush. They are not likely to let two billion dollars in gold slip from their grasp without putting up a certain amount of fight."

"We should be able to establish communication with them, but at this hour it may be difficult to find anyone in authority quickly. Have you any more requests?"

"Just one. Sir, do you know where we are?"

"If you are on or near an island and the Egyptian aircraft carrier, you are at forty-six degrees south, fourteen degrees east. The island is San Juan de la Trine."

"Thank you. Oh, by the way, sir—we were able to save the airplane we came in."

"Very good. Keep me informed."

Kuryakin disconnected, and Waverly signaled his New York office. The operator there answered immediately.

"Get me the highest available official in the Egyptian High Command. I know it's three o'clock in the morning there—wake them up. Call me back as soon as you have the connection."

The Thrush helicopter handled very smoothly under Napoleon's hands as they swooped over the beach and clattered across the half-mile of water separating them from the ship.

He leaned back as Illya put the transceiver away and shouted over the noises of the motor, "Hey, this is fun! No wonder you always want to handle the controls."

"When we get back to New York you can take the qualifying test. Slow down, now—here comes the ship. You'd better set down on the flight deck."

"Right out in the open?"

"*Toujours l'audace*, as you said a few minutes ago. Besides, they certainly won't be expecting *us;* they'll think we're somebody important from the island."

"And come running out to greet us with an armed honor guard."

"Besides, frankly, I wouldn't trust you to land this on anything smaller with as little practice as you've had."

"For shame, Illya. Don't you know that I can do anything? It says so in my contract."

"All right, Napoleon, but it says in *my* contract that I can live forever, and I don't want to make a test case just at the moment. The flight deck."

"The flight deck," Solo agreed resignedly.

The landing was fairly neat after all—they didn't hit hard enough to bounce, and Napoleon feathered the blades like an expert. He threw the engine into idle, and bounded out of the cockpit ahead of his partner, calling loudly for the Captain.

"There has been an explosion on the island," he snapped to the nearest crewman as he imagined an important Thrush would, "and your orders must be overruled for the time being. Bring us your Captain."

Without looking back the two U.N.C.L.E. agents stalked across the wide bare deck towards the control structure. They were almost to the hatch when they heard footsteps trotting up behind them, and a voice said sharply, "What does this mean? My orders were to unload the cargo as quickly as possible and return . . ."

Napoleon wheeled neatly and faced the Captain over the barrel of a leveled automatic. "Your orders have been overruled," he said simply. "Now you will *not* unload the cargo. Instead you will order the entire crew to battle stations, and prepare to resist any attempt to take over the ship and its cargo by force."

The Captain froze where he was, one foot raised for another step. Slowly he lowered it to the deck. His face showed recognition of them as his rescued prisoners. "That will be difficult," he said harshly, "since it appears you have already done exactly that."

Napoleon shook his head. "Only for your own good," he said. "In a matter of minutes you will receive orders from Cairo to coöperate with us. But even sooner those men out there"—he gestured towards the island with his free hand—"will receive orders to attack and capture this ship, whatever the cost. If you successfully defend it against them, you will be rewarded as a hero. Right now, since you haven't heard from Cairo, we have taken the liberty of informing you of your superiors' decision so that you may abide by it while there is still time."

"But this is entirely beyond regulations," the Captain began in a thoroughly understandable confusion. "That the High Command should so completely change its mind . . ."

". . . is admittedly unlikely, but nevertheless is true," said Illya. "We are saving you from making a most grave mistake, though it is also true we must use force to do so. We will surrender our weapons as soon as the communication arrives from Cairo."

The Captain sighed and spread his arms helplessly. "As you say. I have no choice in the matter."

They stepped apart and let him pass between them, then followed him to the bridge. And there he stopped.

"Gentlemen," he said, "I am willing to compromise. I will order the preparations for unloading delayed for a period of ten minutes. If in that time my orders are reversed by higher authority I shall do as you suggest. If not, you may shoot me if you will, but with my dying breath I intend to order the mission completed."

"Half an hour," said Illya.

"Twenty minutes."

"Done," said Napoleon. "And what if the intended

recipients of the cargo out there get impatient and try to take it by force?"

"If force is attempted, it will be met with force."

"Good. That's all we ask."

The order was given. A few members of the crew were appraised of the basic situation, and requested not to interfere. They were perfectly willing.

It was a matter of minutes before the radiophone signaled for attention. Illya picked it up.

"What is the meaning of this delay?" it barked angrily. "Proceed with the unloading operations at once!"

"Very sorry, sir," said Illya politely. "The Captain has observed a serious fire in your settlement, and thought it best to suspend operations to allow your men to combat it. There is no great hurry, after all."

"You were ordered to turn your cargo over to us at once," said the voice, rising in pitch. "We have more than sufficient personnel to control the fire and still continue this operation."

"I am sorry, sir. The Captain has ordered the operation suspended."

"Let me speak to the Captain."

"The Captain is otherwise occupied, sir."

The voice became almost incoherent with rage at this, and babbled something about mutiny, piracy, and hanging in irons.

"I'll tell him you said so, sir," said Illya, and switched the receiver off.

"It seems they know all about it," said Napoleon, and his partner nodded.

"I envy them," said the Captain. "Could someone tell me?"

Napoleon took a deep breath. "First, do you know what you're carrying and what it's for?"

"I know what, but not why."

"Before you start the lecture, Napoleon," said Illya, "I think we had best prepare to be attacked. Captain, whoever I just talked to on the ship-to-shore knows that your government will be calling you in a few minutes. Naturally he wants the gold. If he doesn't take it now, he'll never get it. Is this ship fully armed? With anti-submarine devices as well?"

"Yes—fully equipped."

"Order all defenses into operation. Now."

Five more minutes had passed before all stations reported ready. And only one extra minute passed before one of them reported again.

"Sonar—submarine approaching. Bearing three-two-zero degrees, depth ten meters, range twelve thousand meters and closing."

The Captain looked at the pair of U.N.C.L.E. agents for some ten seconds, then bit at his lip and picked up a microphone. "Ready three anti-submarine missiles. Track, and hold fire."

Suddenly two transceivers twittered, and Illya picked his from a shirt pocket. "Kuryakin," he said.

"Mr. Kuryakin, there is monumental confusion at the High Command. They were apparently informed immediately by a monitoring station when the Wheel ceased transmission, but no creative action has come from them yet."

"Can you offer us any other aid? The ship is about to be attacked, and Thrush might be able to marshal more force than we can stand off. It would be easy enough for them to salvage the gold from our hulk."

The ship-to-shore phone buzzed. Napoleon gestured with his automatic, and the Captain picked it up.

"One moment, sir," said Illya softly to his boss.

The same voice they had heard before spoke, but it was no longer angry. It was cold, and hard. "We have a loaded submarine pointed at your ship," it said. "Unless you begin unloading your cargo at once, we will torpedo you and remove it from the sunken wreck."

The Captain's finger hesitated over the push-to-talk switch, and then he picked up another microphone.

"Missile Control," he said. "Fire one and two at the established target."

One speaker acknowledged as the other speaker clattered angrily, "Captain, answer us! You have one minute!"

They couldn't see the missiles launched, but suddenly the smooth silence of the sea erupted in a furious boiling blast some two miles away. A moment later a second ball of fire flared at the same spot. And silhouetted in the midst of it, photographed on the retinas of the watchers by the explosive flash of the second warhead, was the black outline of a submarine, half out of the water at an impossible angle. And in that moment they saw it break in half as it began to fall back. Then there was a third flare as the armament of the submarine detonated.

No one moved on the bridge until the three concussion waves shook the windows and the distant surface of the sea subsided.

The Captain squeezed the handset of the ship-to-shore, and said, "Pardon the interruption. You were saying that we had one minute?"

The machine remained silent.

"Mr. Kuryakin! Mr. Kuryakin!" a thin metallic voice whispered in Illya's hand, and he lifted it to his ear and answered.

"What on Earth is going on there?" Waverly's voice demanded.

"We have—ah—just reduced the threat, sir."

"Good. How much remains? We can have a flight of SAC bombers to you in a matter of hours. Four hours, if you can hold out that long."

Napoleon had restored his automatic to its holster sometime during the excitement, and now he spoke to the Captain. "Sir, check with Fire Control."

The intercom sounded over his last word. "Sonar clear, sir. Radar reports two small aircraft approaching."

"Ready anti-aircraft. Engine room—"

"Here, sir."

"Get engines up to full speed as soon as possible. Helm—"

"Here, sir."

"Prepare to put about to a course of three-five-zero. Mr. Kuryakin—"

"Here, sir," said Illya automatically.

"Tell whoever you are in communication with that we will want those bombers to fly escort for us until our own Egyptian forces can take over the position."

Illya spoke to Waverly, and received assurance.

The ship's intercom buzzed. "Communications room. Signal from the High Communications room. Signal from the High Command for Captain in maximum security cipher."

"Read it off."

"Cancel all operations and return to base. Do not, repeat, do not complete delivery of cargo under any circumstances."

"Captain," cut in another voice. "Aircraft approaching at two thousand meters."

"Fire only if we are fired upon."

"Yes, sir."

"Communications—send off the following in clear text. *Proceeding home flank speed. Send full protection to relieve American task force as soon as possible."*

A shuddering jar shook them as the anti-aircraft cannon began to fire. The engine room telegraph rang, signaling ready, and the helm was put about.

"Damage Control here. Both aircraft fired high-explosive rockets; one hit. Number three battery damaged. Both aircraft destroyed."

"Fire Control report."

"All clear, sir, unless they have big guns on the island."

Napoleon touched Illya's arm and spoke softly. "I think the military might by which we are surrounded will be capable of handling things from here. Unless you're particularly interested in watching naval operations I suggest we get out of the way and go below. Besides, you still haven't guessed my 'W.' "

They started out the door from the bridge, and walked calmly past and among the various running figures of sailors on their ways to or from posts, as Illya began, "I've established you're a literary figure and American. So you were the Town Crier of the Air?"

"Too easy," said Napoleon. "Not Alexander Woolcott."

"All right. Did you . . . whoops!" A short sailor with a bristly moustache ducked between them and scurried off.

"A lot of people are killed in traffic every day," said Illya philosophically. "Now, where were we?"

"Not Alexander Woolcott."

"Right. Now, did you collaborate with . . ."

The two of them turned a corner, and were gone.